" You're Going To Ask Me To Be Your Mistress. I Swear, Rich Men Are All Alike."

"What an interesting mind you have," Max said. "But no. That is not the plan."

He had looked surprised when she leveled her accusation, so she'd apparently been wrong about what he was up to. She couldn't imagine anything else, though, that he would need to pay her money for.

"Then what?" Janine asked.

"Why, I want to hire you to be my wife."

Dear Reader,

In the second REASONS FOR REVENGE book, you're going to meet Janine and Max.

I probably shouldn't admit this, but Max Striver is one of my favorite heroes ever. He was so fun, so arrogant, so very British that I just adored spending time with him. And introducing him to Janine, an American woman with plenty of attitude, just made this story sing for me.

Writing a book about an island paradise in the middle of winter is always a good thing! Of course, California doesn't do winter like the rest of the world, but I really enjoyed my imaginary trip to the islands. In designing Fantasies, I built a place I would love to stay—of course, I also added a lot of little things I've personally experienced while on vacations.

Though my favorite kind of trip is driving down back roads in Ireland and Scotland, a beautiful tropical island has plenty of appeal, too!

So come back to Fantasies Resort. Visit with old friends, meet new ones and be sure to order the house margarita. It's not to be missed!

Happy reading!

Maureen

MAUREEN CHILD

SEDUCED BY
THE RICH MAN

Silhouette

Desire

Published by Silhouette Books
America's Publisher of Contemporary Romance

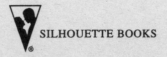 SILHOUETTE BOOKS

ISBN-13: 978-0-373-76820-2
ISBN-10: 0-373-76820-6

SEDUCED BY THE RICH MAN

Recent books by Maureen Child

Silhouette Desire

Society-Page Seduction #1639
*The Tempting Mrs. Reilly #1652
*Whatever Reilly Wants #1658
*The Last Reilly Standing #1664
**Expecting Lonergan's Baby #1719
**Strictly Lonergan's Business #1724
**Satisfying Lonergan's Honor #1730
The Part-Time Wife #1755
Beyond the Boardroom #1765
Thirty Day Affair #1785
†Scorned by the Boss #1816
†Seduced by the Rich Man #1820

Silhouette Nocturne

‡Eternally #4
‡Nevermore #10

*Three-Way Wager
**Summer of Secrets
‡The Guardians
†Reasons for Revenge

MAUREEN CHILD

is a California native who loves to travel. Every chance they get, she and her husband are taking off on another research trip. An author of more than sixty books, Maureen loves a happy ending and still swears that she has the best job in the world. She lives in Southern California with her husband, two children and a golden retriever with delusions of grandeur.

You can contact Maureen via her Web site www.maureenchild.com.

To Romance Readers everywhere.
Thank you all for your support. Without you,
we would have no one to share our stories with.

One

Max Striver picked up his drink and let his gaze sweep the room. The club at Fantasies resort was packed with people drinking, laughing, dancing. The music was loud, and colored lights speared from the ceiling onto the writhing mass on the dance floor. A wall of windows overlooked the ocean and a bright moon spilled out of a black sky.

He leaned one elbow on the bar and took a sip of his single-malt scotch, letting the smooth liquor slide down his throat in a wash of heat. It had been so long since his last vacation, he felt out of place in the room full of partying people. And that wasn't a feeling he was comfortable with. Maybe it had been a mistake to come at all. Maybe he should have stayed in London.

He smiled to himself. But the chance to steal away his old friend and competitor's executive assistant had just been too appealing to ignore.

Still, he'd had no actual hope of hiring Caitlyn Monroe away from Lyon Industries. The woman was too loyal. But it had been fun to torment her boss, Jefferson Lyon. Max took another drink and laughed at the mental image of finding Jefferson sleeping on a chaise beside the pool that morning. Seeing the great Lyon brought so low was entertainment enough to keep Max chuckling for a long time.

"What's so funny?"

Max shot a look at the brunette sitting two seats down from him at the bar. Her dark brown hair was short and spiky and her big brown eyes shone. Her skin was the color of warm honey and her body looked curvy under a pale green tank top and white shorts.

His own body tightened as he felt a stir of pure sensual interest. "Just thinking about a friend," he said.

"And this friend's funny?"

"Not purposely," Max admitted, then asked, "Are you alone tonight?"

She shifted on the high red cushioned bar stool and swiveled it around until she was facing him. Tipping her head to one side, she smiled. "I was."

Intriguing, he thought. He liked a woman who was up-front and not afraid to let her interest in a man show. He liked even more that his own interest was spiking. He'd been spending too much time with work lately.

Hell, it'd been months since he'd had a damn date. But that looked as if it was all about to change.

"Can I get you another drink?"

She glanced at her nearly empty glass, then back at him. "I think that would be a good start."

He signaled the bartender, then speared his gaze into hers. "Would you like to dance while we wait?"

She smiled at him and he loved the way her mouth moved.

"Another good idea," she said and slid off the stool.

As if prearranged, the music shifted from pulsing rock to slow and smooth. Max guided her through the mass of people to a shadowy corner of the dance floor and pulled her into his arms. She fit against him just right, the top of her head hitting at his chin level. And when she swayed into him, Max felt his blood start to pump.

It had been far too long since he'd been with a woman. Far too long since he'd allowed himself a chance to relax.

The music poured over them in a silky wave and she tipped her head back to look at him. "I like your accent. British?"

His arm tightened around her waist. "Yes. You?"

"California."

That explained the lovely tan, he thought and stared down into her deep, dark eyes. "And what brings you to Fantasies?"

"My friends." Janine Shaker felt a ripple of something hot and swirly move through her. That accent of his was really doing a number on her hormones. Or maybe it was just him. Tall, with broad shoulders, a squared-off jaw and black hair that was long enough to brush across the top of his collar, he also had eyes the color of chocolate and a mouth that just begged to be kissed.

Oh, boy.

"So, not alone then."

"My girlfriends," Janine clarified.

She'd come to Fantasies with her two best friends, Caitlyn and Debbie. It had been her idea, though heaven knew, she couldn't really afford this trip. But she and her friends had *all* been dumped by their fiancés over the last few months and this trip was supposed to be a life-affirming-screw-men kind of thing.

So Janine had taken the money she'd put aside for the wedding that had never happened and splurged it on a three-week trip to Fantasies. She'd go home broke, but she'd worry about that later.

At the moment, a man who was the perfect distraction had his arms around her and that was all she wanted to think about.

"Girlfriends, eh?" He smiled down at her and tightened his grip around her waist. "I'm relieved to hear it."

"Are you?"

"Oh, yes."

Seriously, that accent seemed to ripple up and down her spine with delightful results. She was probably making a mistake. Heck, she was sure of it. But she'd lived most of her life being a good girl. Doing the right thing at the right time. Never taking a risk.

And still her world had imploded around her.

Maybe it was time to stop being careful.

At least while she was at Fantasies. After all, the very name of the resort conjured up all kinds of wonderful images.

"Are you flirting with me?"

He thought about it for a moment, then grinned. "Yes, I believe I am."

"Well, good," Janine said. "I think I like it."

His hand on her back slid up and down in a slow motion that might have been considered soothing, except for the flash of heat zipping through her body. "Then we're well on our way to a beautiful new friendship, aren't we?"

"Is that what you're looking for? A friend?"

One dark eyebrow lifted. "For the moment."

"And after this moment?"

"Let's be surprised."

Wow. He really was good at the flirting thing. A quiet but insistent voice in the back of her mind whispered a warning that a man like this wasn't one to take chances with. He was too gorgeous. Too smooth. Too…everything. But it wasn't as if she was looking for forever, was it? She'd tried that with John Prentiss, her former fiancé. She'd believed all of his lies. Believed him when he'd promised to love her forever.

She'd believed right up until the moment three days before their wedding when he'd disappeared, leaving behind only a note that read *Sorry, babe. This isn't for me.*

So she was through with love. But that didn't have to mean she was through with men. She was here. On vacation. In the splashiest, sexiest resort in the world.

Was she really going to lock herself up in her tiny room and be a good girl? Or was she going to do just what she'd told Caitlyn and Debbie they should *all* do? Find a gorgeous man and have mindless, meaningless sex?

With the feel of this man's arms around her, Janine knew exactly what she wanted to do.

When the music stopped and shifted into another drum-driven number that had everyone on the floor jumping into action, Max steered her through the crowd, back to the bar and their waiting drinks. He sat down beside her and said, "I propose a toast."

"To what?" She picked up her drink.

He clinked his glass gently against the rim of hers. "To possibilities."

"I can drink to that," she said and did.

"Are you going to tell me your name?" he asked, his beautiful brown eyes looking directly into hers.

She thought about it for a second, then shook her head. "I don't think so."

"Why not?"

"Because," she said, swallowing her trepidation with a big gulp of her Cosmo, "if we introduce ourselves, then this becomes ordinary. No names means no expectations."

He reached out and stroked the top of her thigh with the tips of his fingers. Goose bumps raced across her skin and she shivered in response.

"No names, then," he agreed, leaning in closer to her. "So, mystery woman, would you like to join me for a walk on the beach?"

"Yes," she said, still shivering at the soft touch of his hand on her leg, "I really would."

The beach was nearly deserted, and the music from the club floated on the cool ocean breeze. Stars flickered on a blanket of black and the moon's pale light shone down like a wash of silver.

As romantic settings went, Janine thought this one was an A-plus.

She should have been nervous. After all, this wasn't like her in the least. Taking long, romantic walks at night on a beach with a perfect stranger. And yet, all she felt was the quickening of expectation. A flicker of heat inside that was as dazzling as the look in his eyes.

"How long are you here for?" he asked and his deep voice was almost lost in the sigh of the wind coming off the ocean.

"Three weeks," she said. "You?"

"I don't know." He stopped, stared out at the water and tucked both hands into the pockets of his slacks. "Coming here was a whim."

She bent down, picked up a broken seashell and fingered it for a moment before tossing it into the incoming tide. "Nothing you have to rush back to in your life?"

He glanced at her and smiled. She really did have an amazing mouth. "Not particularly."

"Must be nice," she said, staring out at the sea. "I practically had to give blood to get my boss to agree to three weeks off."

"What do you do?"

She glanced at him and plucked windblown hair out of her eyes. "I'm a floral designer. You?"

"A little of this. A little of that." He reached out and tucked a strand of her hair behind her ear.

"Well, that was vague," she said.

"Do you really want to discuss our careers?" he asked.

"I guess not," she conceded. "But at least tell me you're not some jewel thief or something."

He laughed and the sound rolled out around her.

"No," he said. "Not a thief. Just a businessman, I'm afraid."

"There are worse things to be," she said, thinking of John Prentiss…liar, thief, con man.

"Besides," he said, "isn't talking about our work the same as exchanging names?"

"No. Work's generic. Names are specific."

"Ah, rules to this, then."

"Aren't there rules in everything?" She looked up at him briefly, smiled, then turned her gaze back on the ocean.

"Should be," he conceded. "Though I confess, I'm enjoying the mystery you suggested."

"Why's that?"

"Because," he said on a sigh, "there aren't nearly enough mysteries in the world."

When he took her hand and pulled her into the circle of his arms, she went willingly. Eagerly. He dipped his head low, tasted her mouth once, twice, and then devoured her.

Janine felt all of the air rush from her lungs and her heart pounded frantically in her chest. His kiss was electric. Dazzling. She felt every cell in her body leap to attention and shout for mercy.

But she didn't want him to show mercy. She wanted him to touch her, taste her, hold her.

She didn't care what his name was. Didn't care that she knew nothing about him. Didn't care that only hours ago, she hadn't known he existed.

All that mattered now was his next touch. His next kiss.

His tongue parted her lips and she opened to him. Wrapping her arms around his neck, she held on tight even as she went up on her toes to meet his advances. His arms vised around her body, pulling her close enough that she could feel the pounding of his heart against her own.

His hands moved up and down her back next, sliding over her clothes, slipping beneath her shirt to caress her bare skin. Every touch inflamed; every stroke made her want another.

He kissed her deeply, passionately and Janine's head spun. She'd never felt anything like this. Hadn't known she *could* feel like this. She trembled and moaned gently when he tore his mouth from hers to rake his teeth and tongue along the line of her throat.

"Lovely," he whispered against her skin, "just lovely. I must have you. Now. Now."

"Yes," she said, tipping her head back so that she could afford him greater access to her body. She wanted his mouth on her, his hands on her. She wanted to feel his body push into her own and she wanted, more than anything, to experience the wild rush of an orgasm ripping through her system. Because she had a feeling this one was going to be a beaut.

He groaned deep in his throat and his hands slipped beneath her shirt, lifting it up and off her too-warm body. Instantly, the cool ocean wind slid across her skin, and became just another sensation whirling together her mind, her blood.

Bending low, he took first one pebbled nipple into his mouth and then the other. Janine could hardly draw breath. She couldn't make herself concentrate on even *that*. All she could focus on was the feel of his hands and his mouth. The rush of her senses, the pulse of her heart.

One corner of her mind screamed at her that they were too close to the resort. That someone might wander down this deserted beach and stumble across them. But a part of her found that thought exciting. And she cringed away from that admission.

The simple truth was, though, that she didn't care where they were. She knew if she didn't feel him on her, in her in the next few minutes, her body was going to explode.

Stepping back from her, he lifted his head and glanced around them, assuring himself that they were still alone. Then he tore off his shirt, spread it out on the sand and lowered her onto it. The cool of the cotton felt good against her back, and when he undid the button and zipper of her shorts, Janine lifted her hips, helping him to rid her of the clothes that felt too tight, too uncomfortable.

The wind stroked her naked body and only made her feel more wanton. More wicked. She'd never been the kind of woman to do something like this. And now that she was, she found she *liked* being this kind of woman.

She stared up at him as he quickly shed his clothes, then knelt between her thighs. His hands roamed up and over her body, tweaking her nipples, sliding over her skin, dipping down into the warm cleft between her legs. He touched her there, intimately, and Janine jolted, hissing in a breath.

He loomed over her until all she could see were his eyes. The depths of them. The glittering shine of a hunger as fierce as her own.

Reaching up, Janine cupped his face in her palms and pulled him down for a kiss. She opened her lips for him; her tongue met his and they tangled together in a furious dance of desire and pleasure. She sighed, heard the heavy sound of it and did it again. Perfect. He was perfect.

She was still kissing him when he plunged his body into hers. Hard and thick, he claimed her, delving in and out of her heat with a passion that stole her breath. Again and again he took her, pushing her higher, faster, than she'd ever been before.

The quickening of her own desire enflamed her and Janine lifted her hips into him, over and over. Meeting each of his thrusts with a wild abandon that took him deeper and deeper inside her.

"I have you," he said, his voice tight with need that still crouched between them like a hungry tiger. "And I want more. I want *all*."

She gave him everything she had and took from him the same. His body pumped and hers kept pace. She raced with him to the precipice that nestled just out of reach.

So close, she felt it. So very close to the edge. Her nails scored his back, digging for purchase as if holding on to him was the only thing that mattered. And in that moment, it was. It was everything.

Janine felt the first spiraling flex of her muscles and knew what was coming. She braced for it, and still was unprepared for the gut-clenching, overwhelming rush of sensation crashing through her. She held on tight and groaned as she took that wild ride into oblivion.

And a moment later, he buried his face in the curve of her neck and followed, his hoarse shout muffled against her skin.

A moment later, Max came back to himself and couldn't believe what he'd done. He'd taken her with no thought to their surroundings. No thought to safety.

He was still buried deep within her hot center and he knew he should be feeling bad about all of this. But he just couldn't manage to.

Instead, he wanted her again.

As fiercely as he had the first time.

"That was—" she stopped, took a deep breath and exhaled again before finishing "—never mind. I don't even have a word for that."

"Nor do I." He smiled and shifted on her, pleased when her eyes closed and a sigh slipped from her mouth. His body was hard and ready again, and from her reaction, he knew she was feeling the same need.

Music from the club drifted down to them and that was enough to make Max say, "I'm not finished. But I'd like to suggest we adjourn to my room."

She licked her lips, sighed a little and said, "Oh, yeah. Good idea."

Two

H_e opened the door of the Presidential Suite and Janine tried not to gasp.

Fantasies was great, no question, but she had reserved one of their smallest and least expensive rooms for herself. This…she couldn't even take it all in.

Walking past him into the living area, she was struck first by the wall of tinted windows that overlooked the ocean and the beach below. The view seemed to go on forever. The carpet was thick enough for her feet to sink into as she turned in a slow circle, admiring the rest of the place.

Crystal vases filled with bright flowers rested on top of glass tables. Bright red couches and chairs created conversation areas at each end of the room and there was even a fireplace—she was guessing more for ambience than necessity. Soft puddles of lamplight shone in the darkness and she spotted a door on either side of the room. Leading to bedrooms, no doubt.

She shivered as he wrapped his arms around her, and she felt the warmth of him seep into her bones. "Amazing place," she said, leaning her head back against his chest.

She heard the smile in his voice when he said, "It'll do until something better comes along."

Turning her head slightly, she looked up at him. "You sure you're not a jewel thief?"

He laughed and she caught the sparkle of delight in his eyes. "Very sure. Just a boring businessman, as I told you."

"Business must be good," she muttered.

His arms dropped away from her and he moved silently to a bar tucked into a corner of the big room. "Well enough."

"Wow. Just got cold in here," she said, reacting to the sudden chill in his tone as much as his abrupt absence.

He flicked her a glance and for a moment, she saw wariness in his eyes, then it was gone. "Sorry. I just don't feel like talking about—well, to be honest, I don't feel like talking at all."

"Me, neither." Janine walked across the room and sat down on one of the red cushioned bar stools. "Boy, the guy who owns this place really does like red, doesn't he?"

The gorgeous man pouring her a glass of wine smiled. "Does seem to be a theme."

"Do you know him?"

"I beg your pardon?"

"The owner. Do you know him?" Janine took the wine he offered and tasted a small sip. Cold and delicious, the wine was, naturally, perfect.

"As a matter of fact, I do."

"Thought you might," Janine muttered. After all, rich guys tended to hang in packs, didn't they? At least, John always had. Of course, as it turned out, John hadn't actually *been* rich. He'd only been pretending to have money. Just as he'd pretended to love her.

He lifted his own glass of the pale gold wine and took a drink before setting it down on the bar top again. Laying both hands flat on the gleaming wood surface, he looked at her and said, "Before this goes any further, we should talk about what happened on the beach."

Janine squirmed a little on the stool. Doing it was one thing, talking about it another. "Why?"

"Because we took no safety precautions."

Six simple words with the power to rock her world on its axis.

"Oh."

"Yes," he said, picking up his wine for another taste. "Oh."

"Well." Janine thought fast. Surprising actually, since her stomach was suddenly full of lead balls, rolling around erratically. "First off, I can tell you I'm healthy."

"Nice to know. As am I. However, there is an even bigger question to be concerned about."

"Yeah." Okay, lead balls a little bigger now and clanking together in the pit of her stomach, making her sorry she'd had such a big lunch. But she took a deep breath, and said, "We'll just have to wait and see, I guess. But it'll be okay. I'm sure. It was only the one time."

One black eyebrow lifted high on his forehead. "I wonder," he mused, "just how often that line of reasoning has been employed over the centuries."

"Wow. When you're worried, you sound way more British."

"I suppose I do. Still, as you say, we'll simply have to wait and see."

Janine felt like an idiot. She couldn't believe she'd made love with a stranger on a beach with no protection. For heaven's sake. She wasn't a stupid woman. But right now, she felt as though she had a huge *L* stamped in the middle of her forehead. *Loser.* Or maybe an *I. Idiot.*

Her fingers stroked up and down the crystal stem of the wineglass until finally he said, "Unless you want a repeat of our earlier performance, perhaps you could stop doing that."

"Huh?" Her gaze shot to his and found fierce hunger shining at her. And just like that, her worries dissolved into a puddle of want. What in the heck was going on here? She'd never been that into sex. Never really craved it as she did now.

And maybe, she told herself, that was because the men she'd been with before hadn't exactly been world-class lovers.

But her mystery man surely was.

Deliberately, she stroked the stem of the glass again and watched flames flash in the depths of his eyes. He came around the end of the bar, plucked her off the stool and lifted her clean off her feet.

At five foot seven, she wasn't exactly a tiny pixie of a woman, and having a man lift her with such obvious ease was really more of a turn-on than she would have guessed. He swung her up into his arms, looked down into her eyes and said, "This time, we'll do it right."

She linked her own arms around his neck, smiled up at him and said, "I thought we were pretty good the last time."

"Mystery woman," he said, heading for the bedroom, "you have no idea."

As good as his word, the second time had been even better than the first. Thankfully, condoms had been readily available, too. And just when Janine was sure they'd outdone themselves, he took it to another level.

She'd never been more relaxed. More completely and totally sated. Every cell in her body was humming with satisfaction, and when she rolled over and opened her eyes to a stream of sunlight, she didn't even mind.

Then she looked beside her at the empty space on the bed and wondered where her handsome stranger was. The sheets were cool to the touch, so he'd been up for a while. She grabbed a robe he must have laid out for her and slipped into the silky material, loving the feel of the fabric as it skimmed over her flesh.

She left the bedroom, walked into the main room and noticed for the first time that there was a balcony jutting off from the living area. She hadn't seen it in the dark the night before. But now, the sun splashed across the flagstone floor and the scrolled iron railing. There was a glass table set under a red-and-white striped umbrella and sitting at the table, drinking a cup of coffee and staring out at the sea, was her lover.

Smiling, she tasted that word again in her mind. *Lover.* She liked it. It felt decadent. Sexy. And the fact that she still didn't know his name was somehow even more wicked.

He was already dressed, wearing black slacks and a dark blue long-sleeved shirt with the sleeves rolled back to the elbows. He should have looked relaxed, unguarded. Instead, he looked like a prince, surveying his kingdom from atop his castle.

She stepped out onto the patio and he looked up at her, offering a smile. Automatically, he reached for the thermal pot in the center of the table and poured her a cup of rich, steaming coffee.

"Thanks," she said. She took her first glorious sip and added, "You were up early."

He shrugged. "London time I'm afraid. Couldn't sleep, but didn't see the sense in rousing you."

"I appreciate it."

"Have you plans for the day?"

God, he even looks spectacular first thing in the morning was all she could think. His black hair was tousled by the soft wind coming in off the ocean and his deep brown eyes were sharp on her. His mouth, that incredible mouth, was curved into a small smile and her stomach did the twisty thing just looking at him.

"Um, no." What she wanted to do was sit right here. Or maybe sit here for a while and then go back to the bedroom. And then come out here again and watch the waves while sneaking long looks at him. But, what she *should* do, as a caring and concerned friend, was go down and see how Caitlyn was doing after her big blowup with her good-for-nothing boss. "But I should check on my friend. See what she's doing."

"Of course." If he was disappointed, he hid it well. Then he leaned across the glass tabletop and covered one of her hands with his. "But I'll see you later."

It wasn't a question; it was a fact. And they both knew it. Turning her hand under his, she held his hand briefly and said, "Yeah. I think that's a good idea."

"Brilliant." He gave her a smile designed to knock her socks—and whatever other clothing she might be wearing—off. "How will I find you, Mystery Woman? Without your name I can hardly ask at the desk."

She glanced back through the open French doors into the plush suite behind them. Then turning her gaze back on him, she said, "You're a lot easier to find. How about if I meet you here around six?"

"Six it is, then." He gave her hand another friendly squeeze and stood up. "If you'll excuse me, I have some business to attend to. Please, take your time here. Enjoy the view. Have some coffee. There's no need for you to rush off."

"Thanks," Janine said and tipped her head back to meet his gaze. "I will."

He bent down and speared his fingers through her short, wildly tangled hair before dipping his mouth to hers to claim a brief kiss. When he pulled his head back, his eyes met hers. "I'll see you at six."

She watched as he turned to leave. Let's face it, he was a much better view than the ocean. Her heart fluttered and her stomach spun just enough to make her smile. Amazing how a night of incredible sex with a gorgeous man could turn a girl's outlook on life around.

When he was gone, she curled up in the comfortably cushioned chair, lifted her coffee and took a long drink. She didn't know where this was going or how it would end. But for the moment, she was going to stop questioning everything and simply enjoy.

It was a gorgeous day in paradise. She was sitting on a balcony that boasted a bird's-eye view of the world and she had a date with a fabulous stranger.

It seemed the resort called Fantasies was earning its name.

The following day, Max had lunch with Gabriel Vaughn, the owner of Fantasies. They were served at the rooftop restaurant, open only for dinner under most circumstances. But when the owner wanted a private lunch, things changed.

"Saw you with your friend at the bar last night," Gabe said, leaning back in his chair.

Max finished off his coffee and kicked his legs out in front of him, crossing his feet at the ankles. "I saw you, too. Thanks for not interrupting."

"No problem. You looked a little too cozy for interruptions."

True. Max thought back on the night before. After some spectacular sex, he'd taken his mystery woman to the club to dance. And after watching her trim, curvy body move sinuously on the dance floor, he'd been all too eager to get her back into his suite. He hadn't felt like this in years. The sharp teeth of sexual hunger were tearing at him continually. Even now, he wanted her, though he'd had her—over him, under him—only a couple of hours ago.

"So who is she?" Gabe asked.

"I have no idea," Max told him with a wry smile.

"What?"

"Nothing," he said, reluctant to explain to his old friend the silly game he and his mystery woman had been playing. Shrugging one shoulder, he said, "I appreciate the lunch, Gabe. But I've a feeling there's something else on your mind besides just catching up with an old friend."

Gabriel Vaughn was usually the very epitome of unruffled cool. Max couldn't remember a time when his old friend had been as tense as he looked at that moment. Five years ago, when they'd met on Max's first visit to Fantasies, the two men had struck up a friendship that had survived both time and distance.

Gabe sat up, braced his elbows on his knees and

speared his green gaze into Max's. "Actually, there's something going on that has…surprised me."

"And not happily, I see."

"Not particularly," Gabe admitted, then shook his head. "But that's not what I wanted to talk to you about."

"Right then. What is it?"

"Elizabeth."

Max blew out a breath. His ex-wife, Elizabeth Bancroft Striver. The once love of his life and current pain in the neck. "What about her?"

"She's coming." Gabe winced and added, "Her assistant called this morning. Made a reservation in Elizabeth's name."

"Bugger." Irritated, Max scowled thoughtfully as his brain raced through scenarios. There was no chance Elizabeth had chosen to come to Fantasies on a whim. She was coming because *Max* was here.

He'd caught her with a lover more than a year ago and had initiated divorce proceedings almost immediately. He wouldn't stand for being lied to. And damned if he'd keep a woman who would cheat on him. Then, to infuriate him even further, he'd discovered that Elizabeth had married him solely for the Striver fortune. She'd had her lover on the side almost from the get-go.

But for the last few months, she'd been dropping by his office once or twice a week, arranging to "bump" into him when he was out, and phoning him at night to tell him how much she "missed" him. He didn't believe it for a moment, of course, but he knew Elizabeth. She wasn't a woman who enjoyed losing. And that was exactly how she would appear on their divorce papers.

Now, she was pretending to want a reconciliation and, worse yet, she'd enlisted Max's father in her battle strategy.

The old man was of the opinion that you never trusted a woman anyway, so why not stay married to the woman you'd chosen and keep her on a tight leash? Max's father wanted grandchildren and he wanted them now. Plus, he believed that Elizabeth would be the perfect mother for the heirs of the Striver dynasty. Her bloodline was lofty enough to dismiss the annoying adulteress accusations.

"My father probably told her I was here. Isn't that perfect?"

Gabe gave him an understanding smile. "I can have the desk call. Cancel her reservations."

He paused to think about that for a moment. Max appreciated the gesture, but they both knew Elizabeth would never allow that to happen. She would come anyway and make quite a scene, perhaps costing Gabe more trouble than he deserved.

"No," Max said, biting back the annoyance. Damned if he'd give Elizabeth the satisfaction of becoming that important to him again. "Canceling her reservations wouldn't stop her in any case. No point in you losing business over my marital…problems."

Nodding, Gabe ran one hand through his shoulder-length brown hair and said, "Your father is still trying to convince you to take her back?"

Max snorted. "You could say so. He takes the trouble

to tell me at least once a week that 'the devil you know' is easier to handle."

"Some would agree."

"I wouldn't be one of them," Max said flatly. Idly, he straightened up and rested his left foot atop his right knee. Smoothing his thumb over the knife-edge crease on his slacks, he added, "I don't make the same mistake twice."

Something in Gabe's eyes shifted, darkened. "Neither do I," he said in a grim voice.

"We're agreed then. Elizabeth will be arriving… when, exactly?"

"Two days," Gabe said. "Are you going to be staying on, or are you going to be gone when she gets here?"

That would be easiest, Max told himself. Leave, go back to London. Ruin whatever plans Elizabeth was counting on. But that was the coward's way out and Max Striver was no coward. And why the bloody hell should *he* have to leave? Especially when he was finding this vacation so…enjoyable.

No, he wouldn't be leaving. He would find a way to put a stop to Elizabeth's plans. It was there somewhere. All he had to do was find the right way to deal with his ex-wife and convince her once and for all that she had no chance at a reconciliation.

Glancing at Gabe, he said, "You've never been married, have you?"

His friend's features tightened perceptibly before relaxing into their more usual expression of easy good humor. "No. Came close once."

"What happened?"

"The lady changed her mind." Gabe grabbed up his water glass and chugged down half of it as though his throat were on fire.

A story, Max mused. And one his friend had no intention of sharing. But then, a man was entitled to his privacy, wasn't he?

"I only wish that I could say the same," Max said at last after a long bristling moment of silence. "Unfortunately, though, I cannot. But I won't run just because Elizabeth has decided she needs to see the tropics." A small smile curved his mouth. "I'm staying."

"Have to say," Gabe told him, "I'm glad to hear it. Didn't think for a minute that you'd run."

Max gave him a quick smile. "Thanks for that. I'm not looking forward to playing Elizabeth's game though, I must admit."

"Maybe what you need to do," Gabe offered, "is to change the rules of the game on her."

"A good idea in theory. But how?"

"I have every confidence in you, Max. You'll think of something."

"Yes. I will." He had two days to come up with a way to thwart Elizabeth. Max knew his ex-wife. She was beautiful and devious. She wouldn't be put off easily. He would need to be at the top of his game to convince Elizabeth to find greener pastures.

Surely he could find some rich, brainless fool for her here at the resort. One who would be as blinded as Max had once been by Elizabeth's physical charms. Or maybe, he thought suddenly, *he* could find someone for *himself*. Someone to make Elizabeth believe that Max had moved on.

Intriguing idea.

"Max. Isn't that your friend, down there?"

He looked past the railing to the swimming pool below and spotted his mystery woman stretched out on a red-and-white flowered chaise. He stood up for a better view. Her tanned, lithe body looked wonderful in a lemon-yellow bikini. As he watched, she sat up, turned to look at the woman beside her and laughed in delight.

Even from a distance, she looked good enough to make his blood hum and his body tighten. She set her hands behind her on the chaise and leaned back, arching her body into the slanting rays of the hot sun and something inside Max twisted hard.

"Beautiful, isn't she?" he mused.

"Yeah." Gabe stood up, leaned on the railing and stared down at the two women laughing together at poolside. "The blonde with her's not bad, either."

Max only glanced at his mystery woman's companion. "I suppose. I hadn't actually noticed her to be honest."

"Really? I did," Gabe said and the flat, hard tone of his voice told Max he wasn't very happy about that fact, either.

Another story, Max thought, but dismissed it almost immediately. As his gaze focused on his mystery woman again, the idea that had begun to bubble in his brain came to fruition.

The answer to his problems, it seemed, had been in his bed all along.

Three

"You're *engaged?*" Janine's voice hit a note so high even she winced. She told herself there had to be some kind of mistake, but staring at Caitlyn's glowing face and beaming smile, she had to discount it. "Seriously engaged. To *Lyon?*"

"This is huge," Debbie muttered and grabbed for her margarita glass. She took a gulp of the frozen concoction, shivered and set it back down. "You just got *un*-engaged like a week ago, for God's sake."

Janine couldn't believe this. Cait had been down-in-the-dumps miserable when Lyon had left the island a few days ago. Now he comes back and everything's great again? Was it just her, she wondered, or had the world sort of tipped over onto its side?

"I know," Caitlyn said and wasn't able to stop grinning. "But Peter breaking off our engagement was the absolute right thing to do. I know that now. Heck, I knew it when he did it." She picked up her raspberry martini, took a sip and kept on smiling. "I think I'm going to have to thank Peter when we go home."

"You're leaving, then?" Janine asked it and was sorry to think about it.

Debbie's former love had been exposed as a bigamist. Caitlyn's ex-fiancé had broken their engagement because he'd claimed she was in love with her boss. Which, Janine supposed, made him a pretty smart guy, since that was how it had turned out.

Janine's ex, though, was in a class by himself. Even her best friends didn't know the whole story of her dissolved engagement. John Prentiss hadn't only ended their engagement three days before their wedding…he'd stolen nearly every dime she had.

"Actually," Caitlyn said, taking another taste of her drink, "tomorrow, we're going to Portugal for a couple of weeks."

"Ah." Janine nodded. "The business trip you told him you weren't going to go on."

"The very one." Cait grinned. "It's different now. We'll go to Portugal, take care of business, then we're coming back here for a week. When we go home, we'll get married."

"At least your mom won't be so pissed off anymore about missing out on the whole mother-of-the-bride experience." Debbie shrugged and stirred her drink.

"I'll call her tonight," Caitlyn said. "She can plan all she wants to. But she's going to have to do it fast. We want to get married as soon as possible."

"Amazing," Janine said. "I never would have guessed that Lyon would be so damn romantic."

"I'm *so* happy, you guys." Caitlyn sniffled and her eyes welled up.

Janine handed her a napkin with Fantasies scrawled across it in red ink. "Don't go getting weepy. Lyon will think we tried to talk you out of marrying him."

As she'd hoped, Caitlyn laughed. "Coming here was the best idea you've ever had, Janine."

"Amen," Debbie added with another slurp of her margarita. "I haven't felt this relaxed in forever."

"It does seem to be working out," Janine said and leaned back in her chair.

She'd worried about coming, even though staying at Fantasies had been her suggestion. After all, this place was costing each of them a bundle. They were all spending the money they'd hoarded to pay for the weddings that had never happened.

But her friends weren't broke. Janine was. Oh, she still had her condo in Long Beach, California, but the equity was gone, since she'd listened to John and taken out a second mortgage for him to "invest." Turned out all he'd been investing in had been himself.

Still, she thought bravely, she still had her job as head floral designer at a very chic flower shop in the exclusive beach community of Naples. And she had hopes that the police would eventually track John

Prentiss down and squeeze him until he coughed up every last cent of her money.

A sentiment she could drink to. At the thought, she downed the last of her Cosmo and turned her mind away from the man who'd cheated her to the man who was currently lighting up her sex life. If she hadn't come to Fantasies, she never would have met her mystery man. And she never would have known just how incredible she could feel under the hands of a master lover.

So, she thought, well worth the price of the vacation.

"Well," Debbie said, "if Cait's leaving tomorrow, I say we all go to the hotel spa and get the works. Massage, manicure, pedicure, facial."

Cait smiled again.

Janine thought about meeting her mystery man later that evening and decided she could use a little pampering, too. "Great idea."

"You smell wonderful." Max dipped his head, took one of her nipples into his mouth and rolled his tongue across the sensitive tip. She squirmed beneath him and his body reacted in a white hot flash.

"It's the lotion," she whispered. "Or the massage oil. Or maybe the seaweed wrap."

He smiled against her breast and nibbled gently. She cupped the back of his head and held him to her breast, as if silently asking him not to stop. No worries there, he thought and kept his attention solely on the task at hand. He was a man of great concentration and at the moment, his legendary focus was intent on exploring every square inch of her amazing body.

She was a feast for a man. Soft curves and toned muscles, she wrapped her long legs around his hips and silently urged him to take her. He already had, of course. And would again, he thought, every chance he got.

Finding her here at Fantasies had been a gift.

In more ways than one.

He knew everything about her now. Knew who she was, where she lived, how she lived. And he knew that if he played this right, she would be the one to help him thwart Elizabeth.

Max lifted his head, looked into her passion-glazed brown eyes and smiled to himself. That talk was for later. Now there was only this moment. This woman. She was insatiable. Nothing like the cold woman he'd married and divorced. Elizabeth had accepted his lovemaking as a task. One she'd carried out with efficiency if not desire.

But this woman came to him eagerly. This woman opened herself to him and gave as much as she took.

"What're you thinking?" she said and inhaled sharply as he dipped two fingers into her tight, hot center.

His body thickened, tightened until it was nearly painful to keep himself from her. But he wanted to wait. Wanted to watch her eyes as he sent her over. Then, and only then, he would take that ride with her.

"I'm thinking that a woman like you is a treat for a man."

She smiled, then tipped her head back into the

pillows and moaned softly. His thumb caressed one sensitive nub as his fingers dipped in and out of her heat in a rhythm designed to bring her to the edge.

"Inside me," she whispered and licked lips gone dry. "Inside me, please."

"Soon," he said and dipped his head to taste her pulse beat at the base of her throat. "Soon. But first, come for me and let me watch. Let me see your eyes as you take the fall."

She slid one hand to the side of his face. Max turned his head, kissed the center of her palm and stroked her center again.

She choked out a half laugh mingled with a groan and managed to say, "You're killing me here."

"No, mystery woman. I'm *filling* you."

He ached for her. Ached for the feel of his body sliding into hers, her body holding on to him like a tight, slick fist. He wanted nothing more than to bury himself within her heat. But first...

She inhaled sharply and her eyes flew open. He saw the jolt of passionate surprise flicker there. As if her body, even knowing what was coming, was somehow shocked to find it arrive.

Her hands slid to his shoulders and he felt her short, neat nails digging into his skin as the first slam of release hit her hard.

She cried out, unable to help herself. Her hips bucked, her back arched and she stared directly into his eyes as wave after wave of soul-shattering sensation ripped through her body.

And when the last of those ripples were just dying away, Max entered her with a quick, smooth thrust that had her gasping for air. Her legs tightened around his hips. Her arms held on to him tightly, as if her hold on him were the only thing keeping her centered.

He moved within her. Fast, hard, impatient now to feel what she had felt. To go over the edge as completely as she had. To join her in that nebulous half-world of satiation and desire. And as he quickened his pace, he felt her body tighten, her inner muscles flex.

Her hands slid up and down his back adding to the clamoring sensations jolting through him. And when he reached the peak, when he felt her join him at the very precipice, he thrust one last time and sent them both flying.

Janine's hands dropped from his shoulders and her arms flopped onto the mattress. She felt completely used up. Spent. And yet, she knew that given a few moments' time to recover, she would want him again.

Sex had never been like this with anyone but him. She'd never suspected that she *could* experience such complete abandon. He brought out something in her that Janine hadn't expected. And she could only be grateful to him for that.

As he rolled to one side and lay flat on his back beside her, she looked slowly around the plush bedroom. A lamp in the corner threw soft golden light into the shadows. The sheer white drapes hanging across the French doors leading to the terrace that ran the length of the suite fluttered wildly in the breeze sliding in off the ocean.

From the main room came the soft sounds of classical music streaming from the stereo, and the fresh flowers on the chest of drawers scented the air with a sweet spice. It was perfect. Everything about this place, this man, was perfect.

Janine smiled to herself and enjoyed the limp, lovely feeling sliding through her body. Who would have guessed she would find such wonder on a vacation she couldn't afford?

"I'm not done," he said softly from beside her.

She laughed, turned her head on the pillow and met his gaze. "Me, neither."

His amazing mouth quirked at one edge and Janine instantly felt a quick flash of something warm dart through her insides.

He rolled toward her, propped himself up on one elbow and said, "I think it's time we exchanged names."

"Do you?" She wasn't sure how she felt about that. True, she did want to be able to call him something other than Amazing Lover Boy. Especially to his face. But, if they introduced each other, wouldn't the magic be lost?

Then he took that decision away from her.

"I'm Max. Max Striver."

She watched him, savoring the name. The short, sharp name suited him—with his chocolate eyes and hard jaw and that mouth that could quirk in an unexpected smile and kiss her until she wanted to whimper.

Okay, magic not gone.

"I'm Janine Shaker."

He reached out and trailed one finger along her jawline. "I know."

She blinked. "You know? How do you know?"

"It wasn't difficult to discover your name, Janine."

Now the magic was dissolving as quickly as sugar in water. They'd had a bargain. They'd promised to keep their names a secret. "So you cheated."

One shoulder lifted in a shrug. "I changed the rules."

"Typical." Funny just how quickly all those lovely warm feelings could just drain away. Rich men, she should have remembered, had their own ideas on what was fair and what wasn't. Even pseudorich men, like John Prentiss. He'd rewritten the rules every time he'd needed something more from her. And she'd never caught on.

Well, she wouldn't be that slow again.

She sat up, scooted off the edge of the wide bed and looked for her clothes. They'd been in such a hurry, her things were scattered all over the damn place.

"What are you doing?"

She spotted her white lace panties hanging off the arm of a chair and snatched them up. Hopping on first one foot, then the other, she tugged them on and up. "What's it look like?"

"I'm not sure," he said lazily and shifted to drag his robe off the end of the bed. "But if I must hazard a guess, I'd say you were getting dressed."

"Bingo," she muttered, still not finding the pale green sundress she'd worn to dinner with him earlier. "Where's my damn dress?"

"I believe you'll find it in the living area," he said

smoothly with just a touch of—blast him for it anyway—humor.

She shot him a glare at the satisfied tone in his voice and then headed for the other room. Her bare feet sank into the pale blue carpet but she hardly noticed. Neither did she pay any attention at all to the romantic music, the soft lighting, or the table on the terrace, set with champagne for two.

He was only a step or two behind her.

"Why are you so upset? I've told you my name," he said in such a placating tone she wanted to kick him. But first, she wanted to find her shoes. Those pointy-toed high heels would really hurt his shin far more than her bare foot would.

"Yes," she snapped and rolled her eyes when she spotted her sundress tossed across the end of the bar. Oh yes. Now she remembered. He'd undressed her the moment they'd stepped into the suite. Not that she'd minded at the time, of course.

But now.

Now, he'd changed the rules on her. He'd gone behind her back to find out her name when they'd agreed to be sexy strangers. Why? Why would he do it? She grabbed her dress, shimmied into it and while she struggled with the back zipper, asked him outright. "Why did you have to do that? Why'd you sneak around and find out my name? Why'd you have to ruin everything?"

"I really don't see why you're so upset," he reasoned. "Didn't you only a moment ago *tell* me your name yourself?"

"Yes, but that was *my* choice." Why do clothing designers put zippers in the back? Why were they so difficult to do up you needed to find help? Was a single person, alone, supposed to go ask a *stranger* to zip them up?

"You're overreacting." He came up to her, turned her around and quickly zipped her dress, managing to stroke her bare skin with the tips of his fingers as he did so.

It simply wasn't fair that his touch could make her shiver. Make her *want* all over again. As soon as she could, Janine eased away from him and continued her search. All she needed now were her shoes and her purse.

"Overreacting?" she repeated. "I don't think so. We had a deal. I didn't try to find out who you were."

"But I did tell you."

"Sure. *After* you knew who I was." She flashed him a quick, angry glance. Okay, one corner of her mind argued, maybe she was overreacting a little. But she'd been enjoying this. The sexiness of it. The mystery of it. And he'd cheated. He'd lied.

And damn it, she'd had enough of men's lies for a lifetime.

"If you're looking for your shoes," he said from behind her, "I've got them right here."

She whirled around, glared at him and charged. "Hand them over."

"Not quite yet, I think." He held them high above her head, out of her reach, and had the nerve to smile at her. "Janine, I only want to talk to you."

"Uh-uh. Done talking. Shoes. Now."

He smiled and damned if that amazing mouth couldn't make her insides quiver whether she wanted them to or not. "Fine," she snapped. "Talk."

She folded her arms across her chest, tapped her bare toes against the carpet and tilted her head to one side, giving him a look that should have set fire to the deep red robe he was wearing.

"I think this calls for some champagne," he said, completely unmoved by her fierce show of temper.

"I don't want any champagne."

"A pity. But I do and I have your shoes."

"What're you, twelve?"

"If I were, you would have been a very bad girl only moments ago."

She blew out a breath and followed him as he strolled out onto the terrace. Out there, the wind was soft and cool; the ocean glittered beneath a pale moon and stars twinkled like far-off lights hung in celebration.

"Will you please give me my shoes?" She squeezed the words out through gritted teeth.

"In a moment." He kept her heels firm in one grip and motioned her to a chair with the other. "Sit. Have a drink with me. I'll explain everything and then, if you want to, you may certainly leave."

"Why thank you, your majesty." She sneered at him, yanked the chair out and plopped down onto it with her temper still riding her hard.

He smiled again and even chuckled a little as he uncorked the no doubt unbelievably expensive champagne and poured each of them a glass.

"I do enjoy you."

"Isn't that special?" She crossed her legs and reached for her glass. Taking one long drink, she let the bubbles soothe her throat.

"If you'd let me explain," he said, sitting down opposite her. In the moonlight, his dark eyes shone. "I have an offer I'd like to make you, if you think you could refrain from tapping your toes so loudly against the flagstone."

Instantly, she stopped the tapping and took another sip of her champagne. Be reasonable Janine. Be calm. "If I listen to this offer, will you give me my shoes?" She heard herself and realized just how stupid that sounded. But it couldn't be helped.

"Of course." As if to show how relaxed he was, he hooked the heels of her shoes over the scrolled iron-worked railing. "Now, as I said, I found out who you were easily enough."

"Congratulations." She gave him a sneer. "You must be so proud."

His lips quirked again. *Fantastic*. She was amusing him, she thought.

"And, once I had your name, I was able to find out…other things as well."

Her eyes narrowed on him. "What're you talking about?"

"I'm talking about your former fiancé and the fact that he stole from you, leaving you—I believe the phrase is 'in desperate straits.'"

Janine gulped down the last of her drink, set the

empty glass down on the table and slowly pushed herself to her feet. Her temper before had been full of fire and heat. Now, she felt cold. Right down to the bone. Wasn't it enough that John Prentiss had made a fool of her? Did she really have to stand here and have another man throw her mistakes in her face?

"You know what? Screw the shoes. *You* keep 'em."

She turned to walk away from him, but he was already there. Moving incredibly quickly, he grabbed her upper arm and held on tightly. "But you said you'd listen and I haven't finished."

"I changed my mind."

"That's merely your temper speaking." He smiled down at her. "As I said before, Janine. I have an offer I'd like to make you. One that, should you agree, would solve all of your financial problems."

She stared up into his eyes and couldn't believe what she was hearing. Of course, why she should be surprised was beyond her. What did she expect? She'd slept with him the night she'd met him. She'd had sex with him almost continually for the last few days. And she hadn't even asked him his name.

Why shouldn't he think she was cheap and easy? Why wouldn't he expect her to leap at the chance to be his mistress? No doubt, he was used to buying and selling people with a flick of the wrist. And now that he knew how badly she needed money, he figured she was easy pickings.

But darn it, it stung.

"I don't believe this."

"What?" He smiled again and this time, his smile didn't stir a thing inside her. "I haven't made my offer yet."

"And you don't have to," she said, tearing her arm from his grasp and looking at him as though she'd never seen him before. "I can guess all too well what you're going to offer me."

"Is that right?" He gave her a nod. "Well, I'm fascinated. Why don't you tell me what you think I'm going to say?"

"You're going to ask me to be your mistress." When he didn't say anything, Janine was sure she was right. "I swear, rich men are all alike. Whatever you want, you get. Is that it? What's the plan? Set me up in a sweet little apartment somewhere? Visit me twice a week?"

"What an interesting mind you have," he said finally, as he shook his head. "And one day, I'd love to hear your reasons for hating men with money. I'm sure they'll be just as fascinating. But no. That is not the plan, as you say."

He had looked surprised when she'd leveled her accusation, so she'd apparently been wrong about what he was up to. She couldn't imagine anything else though that he would need to pay her money for. Confused now, she fought against her own temper and indignation and finally surrendered to simple curiosity. "Then what?"

"Why, I want to hire you to be my wife."

Four

"Your *wife?*" Janine staggered back a step or two, her balance completely dissolving. But he reached out, grabbed her arm and steered her back into her chair. She sat down gratefully and sipped at the glass of champagne he handed her.

"I can see I've surprised you."

"You could say that," she muttered, setting the glass back down and staring at him as he sat opposite her again. "Why would you need to pay anyone to be your wife?"

His features tightened and that mouth of his briefly flattened into a thin, grim slash. Then he smiled again, though it never reached his eyes. He poured more champagne, shifted his gaze to the ocean, and spoke quietly, in a cool, controlled voice. "Actually, I need you to 'pretend' to be my wife."

"Fine. Question still holds. Why?"

"My ex-wife will be arriving on Fantasies in two days," he said, his British accent becoming more snooty and pronounced with every word. A frown tugged at his features. "She is trying to reconcile with me and I'm afraid I'm simply not interested."

Janine took a deep breath. "And this involves me how?"

He turned his head and those chocolate-brown eyes of his speared into hers. There was calculation there. And determination. "I need you to play the part of my wife for the next two to three weeks."

"Again, I say, why?"

"Because," he said softly, "if I'm already married, Elizabeth will have to search out greener pastures."

Janine leaned back in her chair, crossed her arms over her chest and watched him. "Why not simply tell her you're not interested and to take a hike?"

"Ah, what a clever idea. I wonder why I hadn't thought of it?"

"Sarcasm doesn't suit you."

"Really?" he said, amused again. "I thought I did it quite well. At any rate, I have told Elizabeth to 'take a hike' as you so elegantly put it. She refuses to. She seems determined to win me back. I won't be won."

"I'm getting that." Janine saw the hard flash in his eyes and heard the steel in his voice. A part of her sympathized with him. Not a very big part, but still. "Fine. You've got issues with Lizzie."

He chuckled at the name.

"But I don't see how this becomes *my* problem."

"Not your problem," he said, refilling her champagne glass. "Your opportunity."

She waited, sensing he was going to continue, and she'd rather have all the information before she started firing back.

"As I said, through a few inquiries, I was able to ascertain that you've had some financial difficulties lately."

Now it was her turn to laugh shortly. "Difficulties. Yeah. I guess you could call it that."

"Your former fiancé stole from you, taking, I believe, most of the equity in your home and then disappearing shortly before your wedding."

"How did you find out all this?"

He shrugged. "It wasn't at all difficult, I assure you."

"Meaning money talks."

"Actually," he corrected with a smile, "it sings and dances."

"I'll bet." She knew he was right, of course. Hadn't she seen enough proof of it from the customers at the flower shop where she worked? The rich and spoiled always got what they wanted. Enough money could smooth any path.

But she really didn't like knowing that her own life, her own privacy and secrets, were open game to anyone with a hefty bank balance.

"My point is," he said, cutting into her thoughts, "if you agree to play the role of my loving wife for the next few weeks, at the end of our bargain, I will pay you three hundred thousand dollars."

Janine goggled at him. She actually *felt* her jaw drop and had to wait a few seconds for her brain to recover from the shock and kick back into gear. When it did, she said, "Are you nuts?"

"Not at all," he assured her, sipping his champagne with the air of a man who knew his place in the world and was quite comfortable with it. "I assure you, that sum of money is insignificant to what Elizabeth would be trying for. I believe you lost two hundred thousand dollars to your erstwhile fiancé. This bargain with me would net you a tidy profit. And if I do say so myself, you've already seen that the task would hardly be an onerous one."

She was shaking her head and couldn't seem to stop. This was all so bizarre. So completely out of left field. "I don't even know what to say to this."

"Say yes."

She huffed out a breath, stood up on shaky knees, walked the two steps to the terrace railing and curled her fingers around the cold metal. A cool wind brushed her face and tousled her short, spiky hair. Below her, the ocean rumbled in a continuing heartbeat of sound.

This was crazy.

All of it.

She glanced back at Max and found him staring at her, watching her expression with the idle concentration of a man who was confident of getting his own way. Janine didn't know how to feel about that, either. Was she so predictable? Was he so sure that she would agree to this nutso plan?

"Is it really such a terrible idea?" he asked.

"That's what I'm trying to figure out," she muttered, turning her gaze back to the black sweep of ocean and the sky full of stars.

Then her brain started working through the shock. If she agreed, her money troubles would be over. She wouldn't have to worry about losing her home. She wouldn't have to think about taking on a second job.

And best of all, no one would have to know what an *idiot* she'd been to trust John Prentiss in the first place.

All appealing points.

On the other hand, if she agreed to this, she'd be forced to live with Max twenty-four hours a day for the next few weeks. She'd have to pretend to be in love with him. Not so great a hardship, when you considered how she'd spent the last few days.

Still, if she took money for having sex with him, what did that make her?

She winced at the thought.

God, she'd never believed herself capable of being bought. But here she was, seriously considering just that. Her fingers tightened on the railing. Ordinarily, she would have thrown his "offer" back in his face.

But this was no ordinary situation, was it?

She was desperate, and he knew it. *There* was a hard pill to swallow. She really had no choice. Not if she wanted to keep everything she'd worked for. And he knew it.

Max Striver was like every other rich man she'd ever known. Under the elegant manners and smooth charm, he was basically a sleaze. He manipulated people into doing what he wanted by offering them the one thing they needed.

And damned if he hadn't found the right button to push on her.

Turning to face him, she kept one hand on the railing, as if to steady herself. "Let's say I agree…"

"Happy to hear it."

"This is a pretend marriage. Just to fool Elizabeth."

"Yes."

She nodded, swallowed hard and said, "So then we don't have to let sex be a part of this."

His eyebrows lifted. "I beg your pardon?"

"Well, it's not like Elizabeth will be in the bedroom. We don't have to keep sleeping together just because we'll be 'married.'"

"I disagree. Sex will be a part of our bargain," he said, stretching his long legs out and crossing his bare feet at the ankles. "There's an intimacy between couples who share a bed that is lacking in others. Elizabeth is quite perceptive enough to deduce the difference. And," he added, his gaze locked with hers, "we've already proven that our time in bed together is mutually satisfying. Why would we want to deny ourselves?"

"Uh-huh." She lifted her chin. "But if I let you pay me for sleeping with me, that makes me—" She just couldn't say it out loud.

"It makes you a smart woman," he said tightly, obviously fully aware of her thoughts. "Don't insult us both. I'm not paying you for sex, Janine. I'm paying you a large sum to help me in a difficult situation."

Well, it really did sound a lot better said his way.

"Okay." She nodded, grateful he'd put it like that. "How do I know you'll keep your word?"

His eyes flashed briefly with offense. "Once given, I don't break my word."

"I've heard that before," she said, unimpressed. "From the man who said he loved me and then disappeared with everything I owned."

"I don't appreciate being compared to a thief, Janine."

"And I don't appreciate you dodging the question. How do I know?"

"I'll sign a note," he offered. "And at the end of three weeks, I will have the money wired into whichever account you prefer."

She thought about it and even while she did, she could hardly believe she was actually considering this. She knew that if she was smart, she'd grab her shoes and purse and stomp out of the room. She'd like to tell him she wasn't interested in being his paid-for playmate. She'd like to wipe that smug expression off his face by refusing his offer entirely.

But she wouldn't.

She couldn't.

And he knew it.

While she watched him, Max stood up, walked around the table and came toward her. Even though her mind was a whirling, churning mass of thoughts and emotions, her body responded to his nearness with a quick burst of heat. Oh, the next three weeks were going to be interesting.

"So," he said, a smile on his face, "do we have a bargain, then?"

She inhaled sharply, blew the air out again and nodded. "Yeah. I guess we do."

"Brilliant." He cupped her face in his palms and said, "Well, wife…why don't we seal this bargain with a kiss?"

She scooted back and held out her right hand. "It's a business deal, right? Let's seal it the old-fashioned way."

His mouth quirked, but he inclined his head in a gracious nod, then folded his fingers around hers.

So. Had she just made a deal born in heaven?

Or hell?

Money, as Max had told Janine, did indeed sing and dance.

A couple of hours later, after a few gifts in the right quarters, and the help of Gabe Vaughn, Max was able to get official-looking paperwork, which would be more than enough to convince anyone who might inquire, that he and Janine Shaker were husband and wife.

He stood on the terrace of his suite and looked out at the gloriously bright, sunny day. From below came the muted sounds of laughter and the quiet drift of music. And somewhere in the crowds of people, Janine was telling her friends about her change in plan, packing up her things and getting ready to be his Three-week Wife.

He hadn't had a single doubt that Janine would go along with his plan. After all, she needed money desperately and he was here offering it to her. Of course she would take it. Like any other woman, she was willing to do whatever she had to—to gain access to the Striver fortune.

He glanced at his left hand and the intricately carved gold band he'd purchased at a jewelry store in the village. He had a matching one for Janine—to complete the picture. Irritated that it had come to this, Max idly thumbed the ring on his finger. He didn't like the idea of using one woman to shield him from another. But, needs must. With any luck, this ruse would rid him of Elizabeth. When she found out about the marriage, she would be furious. Furious enough to grab hold of the first unsuspecting male who crossed her path.

Then all Max would have to do was pay off Janine and go back to living his life the way he liked it best.

His way.

Janine would go back where she came from and Elizabeth, hopefully, would be some other poor bastard's problem.

"And the very best of luck to him, whoever he might be," Max muttered.

Gabe came up behind him, stood on the terrace of Max's suite and looked down on the grounds below. "You're set. You're now officially listed in the hotel register as Mr. and Mrs. Striver."

Max shot his friend a quick grin. "Gives a man cold chills, doesn't it?"

Gabe grinned right back, leaned one hip on the railing and folded his arms across his chest. "Seems extreme, arranging a marriage to avoid a marriage."

"Sometimes extreme is the only way to handle things." He took a drink of his coffee and added, "When Elizabeth sees that she's lost, she'll complain to my father and I'll have him off my back as well. Thanks for your help with the paperwork, too."

"Not a problem." Gabe glanced over his shoulder at the world he'd created. "Easy enough to do when you own the damn island."

"True enough."

Gabe pushed his hair back from his face and frowned at Max. "So do you think your 'wife' is really going to be willing to go through with this?"

"She'll do it."

"Why?"

Max looked at his old friend and shook his head. He wouldn't be sharing Janine's secrets. Not even with Gabe. This was a private bargain and it would remain that way. "She has her reasons."

"Okay then. I just hope you know what you're doing."

Max chuckled. "I always know what I'm doing, Gabe. You should know that."

"You should have told us."

"Debbie's right," Caitlyn said and her voice carried a note of hurt. "Damn it, Janine. You should have let us help."

She fought the twinge of guilt. She hadn't told her

friends about John because she'd felt like such a fool. But now she felt like a bad friend.

"There was nothing you could have done."

"We would have tried," Debbie said, frowning at her.

"Exactly," Janine retorted. "And I didn't want you to try. I got into this. I'll get out of it."

"Honey, you don't have to do this." Caitlyn plopped down onto Janine's bed.

"Yeah, I really do." Janine smiled at her friend, shrugged and continued her march between the narrow dresser and the bed, carrying her neatly folded clothes to her suitcase.

She'd finally told both Cait and Debbie the whole truth behind John's canceling their wedding. Since they were such good friends, they'd immediately offered to hunt John down like a dog and beat him to death for her. But when she'd let them in on Max's proposition, they were stunned.

And still trying to talk her out of it.

"We can loan you the money you need," Debbie said from her spot in the only chair in the room. "I mean, I don't have all of it, but between me and Cait, we could—"

"Nope." Janine stopped her before she could finish the offer. "This is exactly why I didn't tell you guys in the first place," she said, looking from Debbie to Caitlyn. "I'm not asking either of you for anything. Besides, you can't afford it any more than I can."

"Jefferson can."

Janine turned her gaze to Caitlyn, who was sitting on the bed, watching her. "What?"

"Jefferson. Janine, I'm marrying the man in a few weeks. I'm sure he'd loan you whatever you needed. All I have to do is ask."

"Don't." Janine scowled and scrubbed both hands across her face. "God, I don't want Lyon knowing I'm an idiot. It's hard enough that you two know."

"You're not an idiot," Debbie defended her instantly. "You trusted a man you thought loved you. What's wrong with that?"

"Plenty, as it turns out," Janine said, but managed a smile. "Thanks, though." Looking back at Caitlyn, she said, "Seriously, Cait. Don't tell Lyon. I don't want to borrow the money from him. I don't want to owe friends. Bad enough I'm in a hole, I'm not dragging you guys down with me."

Cait blew out an impatient breath. "Okay, I can see what you're saying, and to be fair, I've known Max a few years now and he's always been a nice guy. But that's surface stuff. I mean, I dealt with him because of Jefferson's business with him. I don't know how he's going to be to live with—let alone to be 'married' to."

"Well, I'll have three weeks to get to know him, won't I?" Janine moved to the small closet and took down one shirt after another. She laid them out on the bed, then folded them, one by one. "And we're not really married, remember."

"That's the part that worries me," Debbie said quietly. "I just don't think it's a good idea. You're trusting a guy who's hired you to lie to his ex-wife. Not exactly a testament to his reliability."

"He's signing a note," Janine argued. "I'm going to have someone at the hotel business center notarize the damn thing. Trust me when I say I'll make sure he sticks to his end of the bargain."

"I'm not worried about that," Cait said and when Debbie sniffed, she said, "honestly. Max isn't a thief, unlike some John Prentisses who shall remain cursed for all eternity. It's just sort of…creepy all the way around. Don't you think?"

"I'm with you," Debbie told her.

"Well, I can't say I'm feeling fabulous about it, but I've already agreed," Janine told them. "I don't go back on my word, so I'm in this. And look at it this way…Max is a *great* lover—"

"Oh, I so didn't need to know that," Cait muttered.

"Well, I'm intrigued, and a little jealous," Debbie said.

Janine grinned. "There you go. And Max and I get along well enough. How hard could it possibly be to pretend to be in love with him?"

"Guess you'll find out," Debbie said.

"I will." Janine finished packing, took a quick look around her small, viewless room and then zipped her suitcase closed. "I'm supposed to meet him at his room in an hour," she said with a quick glance at her silver wristwatch. "So until then, how about my two best friends give me a real send-off? Margaritas for three?"

"Oh," Cait said, scooting off the bed, "I think this definitely calls for a margarita or two."

"We can think of it as a mini bridal shower," Debbie said and stood up, shaking her head. "We'll toast the bride, worry about the groom and stay close enough to catch you if this blows up in your face."

"That's the spirit," Janine said, forcing a nervous laugh. "To me. The temporary Mrs. Max Striver. God help us both."

Five

"This closet is as big as the room I just checked out of." Janine hung up her shirts, looked at the miles of empty closet rod and almost felt guilty for not having enough things to fill it.

Not Max's problem, she conceded as she shot a quick glance at the other side of the huge walk-in closet. The man had brought enough clothing with him to stock a small exclusive men's shop.

"Aren't you fortunate to have traded up then?" Max said from the open doorway.

He leaned one shoulder against the side of the door and kept his gaze fixed on her until Janine wanted to fidget. Silly really. She'd been naked with the man almost continuously for the last few days. And now she got nervous?

"You're enjoying this, aren't you?"

"Shouldn't the question be why aren't *you* enjoying it?" he countered with an easy smile that tugged at her insides.

"Hmm. Let me think." She ran one hand through her short, spiky hair. "Could it be because I'm being paid to pretend to be married to a man I've only known a few days?"

He shrugged. "Consider it a job, with exceptional fringe benefits."

"No ego problems with you."

"None at all," he agreed.

What had she gotten herself into? There he stood, looking like an orgasm on legs and Janine could feel her insides melting. And she wondered, did he feel anything at all for her? *Did he even like her?* Or was she just a handy tool? In the right place at the right time?

She didn't suppose she'd ever really know for sure.

She walked out of the closet, skirted past him and headed for the suitcase open on the wide bed. "Look," she said softly, "I'm just a little nervous. I've never done something like this before."

"I already know you're not a virgin," he said and humor colored his tone.

"Funny." She flipped him a quick look over her shoulder. "I *meant,* I've never had to act a part before. Pretend to be someone I'm not."

"Haven't you?"

"No. And I don't know if I'll be able to pull it off."

"You'll be fine. I'm not asking you to behave like a duchess. Simply like a woman who's madly in love with me."

"Oh, well then. That makes it much easier." She watched as he pushed away from the wall and walked toward her. Reaching into his pocket, he pulled out a small maroon velvet jeweler's box and opened it.

Janine sucked in a gulp of air. A gold band, wide, thick, intricately carved with leaves and sprinkled with tiny chips of diamond, winked up at her. "Whoa."

Smiling, he took the ring from its bed, lifted her left hand and slid the band onto her finger. It felt heavy. And oddly right. She shut that thought down quickly and instead concentrated on the weirdness of the situation.

"There," he said. "Now it's official."

"Swell. An official lie."

He held up his own left hand and she saw the matching ring on his finger. "We're in this together, Janine. And believe me, it will all work out just as it should."

Her heart fluttered in her chest and her stomach took a nosedive. Suddenly, she was more nervous than ever. Having great sex was one thing. Living here with him, pretending to be his wife, was something else.

"Max…" She shook her head and stared at the ring. "I don't know how to be a rich man's wife. I mean…I don't do operas and fancy restaurants. I'm more the movie-and-tacos kind of girl."

"I love the movies," he said and tucked a strand of her hair behind her ear.

His touch skittered heat through her like buckshot. "And tacos are delicious."

"Uh-huh." She reminded herself to breathe, which wasn't easy since he kept touching her. Why did he have to keep touching her? "But Elizabeth will never believe that a guy like you married someone like me."

He frowned and his eyes narrowed. "Why wouldn't she?"

"Because…" She stepped back, out from under his hand that kept caressing the back of her neck. "Because girls like me don't end up with men like you, Max. We just don't. How many of your friends' wives are florists? How many of 'em live in condos in Long Beach? How many of 'em are still making payments on a four-year-old car?"

"When this is over, you can buy a new car. For cash."

"That's not what I meant." That bubble of nerves in her stomach had suddenly become a roaring, fizzing tide of bubbles, making it hard to catch her breath. "You and I are way too different, Max. Your ex is never going to buy that I swept you off your feet."

"But you did," he said, his voice a low rumble of sound that rippled over her skin. "You absolutely did. From the moment I met you in the bar. I looked into your deep, dark eyes and knew I was lost. You touched me and I fell. I kissed you and knew I never wanted to taste anyone else."

Janine swallowed hard. Her mouth was dry, her palms damp and the bubbles in her stomach frothed and churned. Where was this coming from?

He slid the tip of one finger along her cheek and down to the line of her jaw. His gaze on hers softened. "Your sense of humor, your laughter, your sighs, fill me more completely than anything I've ever known."

"Max…" She was being swept away by a tidal force of something she hadn't expected. Something she hadn't seen coming. She'd had no idea he'd felt like this. No idea *anyone* could feel this way about her. She didn't know what to say. Didn't know what to do.

"You're everything to me, Janine. That's why I married you. That's why I'll keep you."

Her knees wobbled and her head spun. She smiled, took a breath and then blew it out when he spoke again.

"You're *very* good," he said, stepping back from her and giving her an appreciative nod.

"Excuse me?"

"I don't know why you believe you're not a good actress. There's no reason at all for you to be nervous, Janine. You're reacting perfectly." He smiled. "You're the very picture of blushing romance. Excellent job. Now, if you'll just do the same thing in front of Elizabeth, all will be well."

"Perfectly," she whispered.

"Why, if I didn't know better, I would swear that you were wildly in love with me." Max dipped his hands into the pockets of his slacks.

"You were practicing."

"Naturally," he said. "I wanted to prove to you how well this is going to go. I hope you're convinced."

"Oh yeah. I'm convinced." She needed to sit down.

She dropped to the edge of the bed, staring up at him. She looked into his eyes, eyes that only a moment ago had been filled with emotion, and now she saw only cold calculation. What did that say about him?

That he was an excellent liar.

"And you saw how easy that was. Simply look at me the way you just did and Elizabeth will believe everything we want her to."

"Right. Elizabeth." Well, why wouldn't the other woman believe it? Janine almost had. And she *knew* that none of this was real.

Slapping his hands together, he rubbed his palms in gleeful anticipation. "We'll do very well together, Janine. You'll see. Now. Elizabeth is due to arrive in just a day or so. And the woman cannot be counted on to be timely, which means she could arrive earlier than expected."

"So?" God, she felt stupid. Her head was still filled with a romantic haze, and her limbs still felt weak and rubbery. *When* was she going to be immune to good liars?

"So, we must be ready."

"I'm as ready as I'll ever be," she said.

He stepped closer, tipped her chin up with his fingertips and looked into her eyes. "Not quite yet. Before my ex-wife shows up, I'm going to take my present wife shopping."

"Shopping?" She pulled her head back, away from the distraction of his fingers on her skin. "I'm not going shopping with you."

His eyes narrowed and his features went grim. "You agreed to this, Janine. Now I expect you to fulfill your part of our bargain."

"You never said anything about shopping." She'd never liked shopping. Maybe that was an affront to her feminine genes, but to Janine's way of thinking, a mall was practically the seventh level of hell.

He sighed. "As my wife, you'll be expected to dress a certain way. To have certain things."

"I don't want new things."

"A pity. You'll have them anyway."

"You're enjoying this, aren't you?"

The gleam of victory shone in his eyes briefly. "Very much."

"Fine." Janine stood up and lifted her chin, like a warrior princess facing down her executioners. "I made the deal. I'll stick to it. Do your worst."

"You're very brave indeed."

"Like I said, sarcasm doesn't suit you."

"On the contrary," he said, coming to her and tucking her arm through the crook of his. "It suits me down to the ground. Now, buck up, wife. You're about to make quite a few shopkeepers in the village very happy."

"Whoopee."

He'd never had so much trouble spending money on a woman.

In Max's experience, women given free rein to his financial coffers always reacted like a child on Christmas morning. There was glee and greed.

There was neither with Janine.

She went along with his choices, grumbled some about spending so much time in the shops, but never so much as hinted at a choice of her own. She couldn't have been less interested and, despite his best intentions, he was intrigued. She didn't seem to care about his money—beyond the agreed-upon sum he was paying her to go through with this ruse.

In fact, before they'd left the hotel for the village, she'd insisted that they stop at the hotel business office, where he'd written her a promissory note and had gotten it notarized. Though it stung Max's pride that the woman clearly didn't trust him to follow through with his end of their bargain, he could at least admire her thoroughness.

And yet, watching her as she tried on one outfit after another in an exclusive clothing store, he thought she looked more miserable than anyone he'd ever known.

When they were at last finished, he arranged to have their purchases delivered to the hotel and then steered Janine down the narrow village street. He held her left hand in his right, and his thumb idly moved over the gold ring on her finger.

She tried to pull her hand free, but stubbornly, Max just tightened his grip. "We're married, remember? Try to look happy."

She laughed shortly. "Were you happy the *last* time you were married?"

"Hmm. No," he allowed. "But this is different, isn't it?"

"It is for me."

"Me as well," he assured her and caught her when she tripped on a loose cobblestone.

"Thanks." She tipped her face into the wind and he watched as she sighed with pleasure. "You didn't have to buy so much."

"You're the first woman I've ever heard make that particular complaint," he admitted, and glanced down at her.

"Then you're hanging with the wrong women."

"Perhaps." He guided her around a young couple, arms wrapped around each other and oblivious to the world around them. If he felt a pang of envy, it was quickly buried. He'd tried once to find happiness with one woman and it had ended in disaster. "The point is I'm *hanging* around with you, now. What else would you like to do in the village?"

"No more shopping," she said quickly.

"Yes, I guessed as much." And since it still surprised him, Max smiled. "Shall we have lunch, then?"

"Some posh restaurant with a wine list and cloth napkins?"

He smirked. "You prefer paper?"

"Don't look now, but you're sounding snooty and British."

"I *am* snooty and British."

"Right." She actually laughed and he enjoyed the sound of it. "My bad. I forgot. But if we're doing lunch, we're going to a place I found a few days ago. And, it's on me."

One eyebrow lifted. "Really?"

"Don't look so surprised. Hasn't a woman ever bought you a meal before?"

"Actually, no."

"Then I'm happy to be your first."

She led him off down the street and Max could admit, if only to himself, she was his first in many things.

"That won't do at all."

"I'm sorry ma'am, that's the best we can do."

The tall, slim, elegant woman wore a cream-colored silk shirt, pale green trousers and heels that looked as uncomfortable as they did expensive. Her wheat-colored hair was up off her neck and twisted into a knot that was studded with what were probably real pearls.

Janine stood beside Max in the hotel lobby and watched the woman she was willing to bet was his ex-wife as she made the desk clerk's life a living hell. The minute they'd walked in through the front door, Max had stiffened and come to a complete stop.

Now, he draped one arm around her shoulder and Janine could sense the irritation swimming through him. She fought down her own sudden spurt of nerves as she realized that she was about to start playing her role, whether she was ready for it or not.

And a part of her wished she were wearing one of the fabulous new outfits Max had just purchased for her. Because, standing there in a simple red sundress and flat black sandals, she felt severely underdressed for the confrontation to come.

The wide, plush lobby of Fantasies was dotted with people, gathered at the small knots of red furniture placed around the tiled room. Glass tables held crystal vases filled with bright flowers and the walls of windows allowed views every way you turned.

But Janine couldn't enjoy any of it. She was way too busy watching Max's ex-wife. Only a few minutes ago, she'd been laughing. After enduring the forced shopping trip, she and Max had had lunch at a tiny café near the island harbor. The two of them sharing fish tacos, which she'd insisted on, had made her feel more in charge than she had in the exclusive dress shops.

But now, faced with the coldly imperious woman just a few feet from her, Janine was once again feeling way out of her league. And she didn't like it.

"Do *not* call me *ma'am,*" the woman said, her cultured, British voice biting off every syllable. "My assistant arranged these reservations and I was assured of a luxury suite."

"Yes ma'am—I mean, miss," the young clerk muttered, flushing red to the roots of his blond hair. "But you did arrive early and all I have available is a junior suite."

"Do I look as though I would be satisfied with a *junior* suite?" Elizabeth impatiently tapped her long French-manicured nails against the top of the glass registration desk.

"Well gee, Max," Janine whispered, "she's a real sweetheart."

"As quiet and unassuming as ever," Max muttered.

Then he turned his head and looked down at Janine. "Are you ready to begin?"

"As ready as I'll ever be, I guess," she said, instinctively lifting her chin.

"Excellent. Let's bell the cat then, shall we? Before she tears that young man's throat out."

"Remove the people currently in my suite," Elizabeth was saying as they approached the desk.

"I—I can't do that, ma'—miss."

Amazing. Janine listened to the elegant woman issue commands with every expectation of having them followed and wondered how people achieved that kind of arrogance. Were they born into it, or was it something they worked at? Despite the thread of nerves whipping through her, she braced herself. No way was she going to let Max's ex get to her.

The desk clerk was still stammering and looking as though he wished he were anywhere but there. "I'm sorry, really, that's simply impossible, Miss—"

"Mrs.," she corrected. "Mrs. Elizabeth Striver."

"Ex Mrs. Striver," Max said, his quiet, steely voice slicing through the temper-filled air like a sword made of ice.

Elizabeth whirled around, a wide smile on her face that never came close to warming up her cool blue eyes. "Max! You've come to greet me in person. Thank you, darling. That was so thoughtful." Her gaze slid quickly to Janine and then away again. "Max darling, you must help me deal with this person."

Janine watched the kid behind the counter scrape

one hand across his face and she felt a tug of sympathy for him. Then saved the rest for herself. After all, *she* was the one who was going to have to be dealing with the queen of the universe.

"Elizabeth," Max said, "if there is no room for you, you'll simply have to wait."

She pouted prettily and slapped one hand gently to his chest. "Now Max, don't tease. Why, one would think you didn't care."

"One would, wouldn't they?" His voice was thick and tight with repressed anger, and Janine marveled that the other woman either didn't hear it or didn't care enough to pay attention to the warning.

"Well," Elizabeth said, once again glancing at Janine and then away again, as if she didn't want to dirty her eyes by looking for too long, "if it can't be helped, it can't be helped. I'll tell you what we'll do," she said, eyes brightening and mouth curving into a delighted smile as she turned to the hotel clerk. "If my suite's not ready, I'll just stay with my husband until it is. Knowing Max, he has the Presidential Suite. I'm sure there's room for me."

The clerk's eyes got a deer-in-the-headlights look to them as he shifted a glance at Max.

"No, you won't," Max said, with a decisive shake of his head. Speaking directly to the desk clerk, he added, "This lady is my *ex*-wife and she is not to have access to my suite under any circumstances, is that understood?"

"Now Max, don't speak so. This poor man will think

you a very poor husband indeed. And surely you won't sentence me to a life of gritty misery in a junior suite when you've more than enough room for a 'guest.'"

"I don't have the room as a matter of fact," Max said, and ran his hand up and down Janine's right arm, drawing Elizabeth's attention to the motion. "My *wife* and I would prefer to be alone."

"Your what?"

Whoa. Janine felt the frost in the air and wondered if her breath would puff in front of her face.

"Wife."

Now, Elizabeth's blue eyes fixed on Janine and it was all she could do to keep from squirming. Here we go, she thought, gathering up every ounce of nerve she'd ever had. Weird, but she'd never been daunted by the rich and tacky before. She'd gone toe-to-toe with more than one society queen who expected her floral orders to take precedence over say, the rest of the world.

But dear God, if looks could kill they'd have been able to bury Janine right there in front of the registration desk. And maybe there'd be a small, tasteful plaque. Here Lies a Woman who Should Never Have Said Yes to a Rich Man.

"Wife?" Elizabeth repeated and Janine was pretty sure she could actually see icicles forming in the air between them. Oh yes, the next three weeks were going to be a lot of fun.

"Yes, my wife." Max, ignoring Elizabeth's irritation, said, "Janine dear, this is Elizabeth. My former wife."

"Nice to meet you."

"Oh," the cool blonde said, "I'm sure it is." She looked at Max and cooed, "Darling, whatever game you're playing at, I don't find it amusing."

"Oh," Janine said quickly, plastering a phony smile on her face, "it's no game, Lizzie…"

"Elizabeth—"

Janine wrapped both arms around Max's middle and cuddled in. "We got married just yesterday. It was sooooo romantic. Sorry you missed it."

"Oh, as am I," Elizabeth muttered. "Yesterday, you say. Awfully sudden, wasn't it?"

"Max just swept me off my feet, isn't that right, Max?" She blinked innocently up at him and returned the smile he gave her.

"Absolutely," he muttered and dropped a quick, hard kiss on her mouth.

"How very…nice for both of you," Elizabeth said.

"Isn't it?" Janine blew out a breath and said, "I'm really sorry, Liz, but Max just tired me out last night. I think my new hubby and I need a nap."

"Elizabeth," the woman said with a snarl.

"Right. Sorry." Janine shrugged and leaned closer into Max. Looking up at him, she said, "What about it, honey? How's a nap strike you?"

"Brilliant idea, my love," he murmured, stroking one hand up and down her spine. Then he looked at the blonde watching them through slitted eyes. "Elizabeth, good luck with your reservation trouble."

They walked arm in arm to the bank of elevators on

the far side of the lobby and, just as they turned the corner, Janine chanced a quick glance back. Elizabeth was watching them.

And she didn't look happy.

In that moment, Janine knew she was going to earn every penny of the money Max had promised her.

Six

Max waited until they were in his suite before speaking. His temper spiked, settled and spiked again on the elevator and during the walk down the hall. By the time they were in their suite, he was ready to answer all of the questions he expected Janine would have. "Should have known she'd arrive early."

"You could have warned me that she's a witch." Janine dropped onto the deep red sofa and curled her legs up beneath her.

Max glanced at her as he walked to the bar and stepped behind it. "If she were a nice woman, chances are, I'd still be married to her, wouldn't I?"

Janine's eyebrows lifted. "Cranky much?"

He frowned, poured a short glass of scotch and drank

it down like medicine. Then, setting the tumbler back onto the bar top, he looked at her. "She's a way of getting under my skin like no one else."

"Why do you let her?"

"Excuse me?"

Janine shrugged, wrapped her arms around her middle and said, "She's your *ex,* Max. Why do you care what she does or says?"

"I don't." He really didn't. There'd been a time, of course, when Elizabeth had occupied a good deal of his thoughts. Back then, though he hadn't loved her, he had been attracted. Interested. Though that time was long over, he found she could still grate on him. Something like salt in a wound. "Having her a constant thorn in my metaphorical paw is irritating."

"So, why'd you marry her in the first place?"

He poured another drink, then opened a chilled bottle of chardonnay and poured Janine a glass of the cold white wine she preferred. After carrying it to her, he took a seat on the sofa, stared down into the amber scotch in his glass and said, "Many reasons. The main one being her family and mine wanted the match."

"An arranged marriage?" She took a sip, shook her head and said, "Jeez, I knew you were British. Didn't realize you were medieval."

"What's that old saying, *the more things change, the more they stay the same?* Some traditions, shall we say, die hard in England." He sipped at his scotch, then leaned his head against the back of the couch. "Marriages in some circles are, even today, generally more about lineage than love."

"That sucks."

"It does indeed," he said, sliding a look and a half smile at her.

"So why doesn't Lizzie just find some other lineage to lay claim to? Why's she so hot on getting you back?"

He lifted his head, looked at her. "Elizabeth doesn't like losing any better than I do. Her pride took a beating when I insisted on a divorce."

Cradling her wineglass between her hands, Janine watched him for a long moment. "And you really think a woman like that is going to give up and go away just because you have a 'new wife'?"

"I do." He pushed off the couch, shoved one hand into his slacks' pocket and walked to the French doors leading to the terrace. "Because I plan on throwing you into her face at every opportunity."

"Wow. Lucky me."

He whipped his head around and speared her with suddenly hot, flashing eyes. "You agreed to this bargain, if you'll remember."

She held up one hand in surrender. "I know what I agreed to. I'm not trying to weasel out of anything."

"Good." He turned his head back to the terrace doors and the evening beyond. The sun was sliding into the sea, swirling the sky with shades of gold and scarlet that clung to the drift of clouds like brilliant paint on sailing vessels. The first star winked into life as he watched and he forced a calm he didn't feel into his bones. When he knew he could speak without snarling, he said, "There will be no 'weaseling' of any kind. We're both in this to the finish. And by the end of it, Elizabeth will be only a bitter memory."

She sighed behind him and Max almost wondered what she was thinking. But he could guess well enough. He presumed she was regretting stepping into this little bargain. But wishes were useless as he knew only too well. So best she understand now that he wouldn't be releasing her from this task.

Turning his back on the incredible view, he faced the woman who was his temporary wife and spoke softly. "For the next three weeks, you're going to be my wife. That means you will conduct yourself accordingly at all times." He walked toward her, stopped when he reached the sofa and looked down at her. "No more spending your evenings drinking with your friends, or dancing at the club unless I'm with you."

"Now just a minute…" She set her glass of wine on the nearest table and stood up. But even pulling herself to her full height, she was forced to look up to meet his gaze. "I agreed to this, but—"

"No buts." He cut her off neatly, tossed back the last of his scotch and said, "From here on out, who you were is gone. You're no longer a single woman on holiday. Now you're my wife. And you'll do as I say."

She looked him up and down, and then folded her arms across her chest. "You know, Max? If you acted this much of a bastard with Elizabeth, I can't imagine why she wants you back."

He reached out, cupped the back of her head and pulled her close. He ground his mouth over hers in a hard, fierce kiss and he didn't stop until he felt the gentle sway of her surrender. Then he lifted his head, cocked a brow and asked, "Can't you?"

"I knew going in that I was going to regret this," Janine said the following afternoon. "But damned if I knew how much I'd want to kill him."

"Honey," Debbie said, "all of us end up wanting to kill a man sooner or later."

"Yeah, but look at me!" Janine waved one hand down the front of herself, to indicate the deep violet silk dress with the scooped neck and elegant cut. She had diamonds at her throat and sparkling in her ears. Her makeup was perfect and even her spiky hair had been tamed into what looked like tousled curls instead. "He's turned me into someone I'm not. This isn't me. This silk and the makeup and *diamonds*."

"Poor little you. Forced to dress up and wear pretty things. He should be shot."

"Very funny." Janine smirked at her. "Fine. I'm not exactly being chained to a wall, but you know I hate this stuff, Deb. I'm a jeans and T-shirt girl. I don't wear diamonds. Hell, I don't *own* diamonds."

"You do now," Debbie pointed out, with only a slight touch of wistful envy.

"No way. I'm not keeping any of this stuff," Janine vowed. She broke off a small corner of the hot bread sitting in the middle of their table. Popping it into her mouth, she said, "I don't want his damn jewels. Or the stupid clothes. Where would I wear them back home? Can you see me, standing in the flower shop wearing this getup?"

"Actually, yeah. You've always had the confidence to pull off anything." And Debbie'd envied that self-assurance more than once over the years.

Janine blinked, smiled a little and said, "Thanks, but this is so not me."

"Well, if it makes you feel better, give it all back," Debbie said. "I just don't get why you're so pissed off about it. Most women wouldn't complain about a man spending a fortune on them."

Scowling, Janine drank the last of her mimosa and set the glass down again. "I think what bugs me most is Max *expects* me to want all this stuff. Like because I accepted his damn bargain, he can *keep* buying me. That doesn't even make sense, does it? No wait. It does. He gets this look on his face—"

"What?"

"I can't even explain it. It's like tired and bored. We went into those shops and the women there fawned all over him, racing around in circles, trying to sell him as much as they could before he slipped away again."

"Seems natural."

"Yeah, but the looks he gave me weren't. Like he couldn't figure out why I wasn't into it. Like why I wasn't drooling over his credit card."

"He doesn't know you," Debbie said and reached out to pat her friend's hand. Janine had never really cared about money. And Debbie had never understood it. For Janine, all that was important was a home. Having her home and a place to work with the flowers she loved was enough. The only reason she'd accepted this deal with Max was so she could replace what John had stolen, return to her everyday world and not be afraid to lose it.

For Debbie, money was more important—not spending it, squandering it, or lording it over everyone who didn't have it. But she liked knowing it was there, as a safety net. She'd worked hard, had built up her travel agency and had carefully tucked away every spare cent, all to ease the constant, niggling fear that lived inside her. Janine and Cait teased her about it, naturally, but then, neither of her best friends had ever really been *poor.* Had never gone to bed hungry, or worried about not having a place to sleep.

Well, Debbie had and it sucked.

"Max doesn't know you, that's all," she said as Janine continued to glower at the table.

Debbie shrugged, signaled for their waiter and ordered another two mimosas. Champagne and orange juice. People should drink it all the time, she thought. It would seriously improve their dispositions. Of course, it wasn't doing much for Janine's at the moment.

Still, who could blame her? She'd been cheated out of everything she owned by the man she'd thought loved her and then forced to pretend another love, just to try to hold her own world together. A lot of crapola in a very short time. No wonder she was feeling a little less than chipper.

A shame though, Debbie thought, glancing around the crammed restaurant at the well-dressed crowd. They'd come to Fantasies looking for escape and so far, both Cait's and Janine's pasts had arrived to haunt them.

Debbie's mom used to say that bad luck came in threes.

Which, if truth were told, was making Debbie just a little bit nervous.

"If it's that bad," she spoke quickly, more to shatter her thoughts than anything else, "quit. Walk away. He can't stop you."

"That's what you think." Janine leaned back in her chair and folded her arms across her chest, like a petulant child, pouting. "He'd find a way. Besides, I can't quit and you know it as well as I do."

"The money."

"Exactly. I can't risk losing my home, Deb. I worked too hard to get it. So I'll stay with Max and I'll play the part. But that doesn't mean I won't complain about it to you."

"Understood."

Janine blew out a breath, glanced over the railing at the pool beyond the restaurant and shook her head. "I feel like I'm in a play and they keep changing the script on me."

"What do you mean?"

She sat up, braced her arms on the glass tabletop and scowled. "Last night, his majesty informed me, there'll be no hanging with you at night. Or going dancing. I'm his 'wife' and I'll do as he says."

Debbie winced and took a sip of one of the mimosas a handsome waiter delivered. "Did he make you salute?"

"It was close."

"Okay, but you had to know that would be part of it."

"I suppose, just hadn't really considered it." She sighed and picked up her fork to stab at the chef's salad in front of her. "And now I feel guilty."

"About what for heaven's sake?"

"About you. Bailing on you," Janine said. "Cait's off in Portugal with Lyon of all people, I'm trapped with my British jailer and you're on your own." Disgusted, she dropped her fork again. "This was supposed to be a trip for *us*. The three of us. To party. To relax. To have fun, for Pete's sake."

Debbie sighed. Sure she missed hanging with her friends, but she was still enjoying herself. How could she not in a place like Fantasies? Even if she did, every once in a while, feel as though she were being watched.

She shivered a little, rolled her shoulders and dismissed the notion. At the moment, she wasn't feeling anyone's eyes on her and that was good.

"Look, Cait'll be back in a week or two. With any luck, Max's ex-wife will get tired of being snubbed early and we can go back to having fun."

"You think?"

"Why not? Would *you* stick around if your ex was rubbing your nose in his new relationship?"

"I guess not."

"So." Debbie picked up Janine's mimosa, handed it to her, then held her own out, waiting for her friend to clink glasses with her. "Let's keep with that good thought, have a toast to the Queen Witch leaving in a snit and enjoy what's left of our lunch, okay?"

Shrugging, Janine agreed. Their glasses touched with the music of crystal and both of them took long, satisfying drinks. When she set her glass down again, Janine said, "You're right. Maybe, if I play this part well enough, I could actually chase her off faster."

"That's the spirit," Debbie crowed, glad to see a sparkle back in her friend's eyes.

As Janine tucked into her lunch, she started talking, telling Debbie all about the Presidential Suite, about the mountain of clothes and jewelry Max kept heaping on her....

And Debbie heard only about every other word. That creepy sense of being watched was back. It was probably nothing, but it was enough to make her signal for the check and hurry her friend along.

Three nights later, the live band on stage created hot, bluesy music swirling around the crowd gathered in the club at Fantasies. Tables of gleaming oak and sparkling glass dotted the room, circling a wide dance floor that shone beneath winking colored lights.

Candles rested in the center of every table and soft lighting from seashell sconces on the walls kept the atmosphere to a soft glow. Crystal clinked, laughter bubbled and conversation swam through the air with a muted hush that rose and fell with the rhythm of the band's melody.

Janine swept one hand through her softly curled hair and accidentally sent a swag of diamonds at her ear swinging. She'd never get used to it, she thought. Not the glamour, not the lies. Not any of it.

"Mrs. Striver?"

She jolted in her seat, then smiled at the waiter who'd spent half the night hovering near their table. "Yes. I'm sorry. What?"

"I've a message for you, from your husband." He held out a folded piece of paper and when Janine reached for it, the waiter smiled. "May I freshen your drink?"

"Um, sure. Marg—"

"Margarita on the rocks, no salt," he said quickly. "I remember."

She nodded as he moved off into the crowd. Just one more thing she couldn't seem to get used to. As the "wife" of a very rich man, she had the entire staff of Fantasies practically leaping to attention whenever she was around. No one could do enough for her.

"Just weird," she muttered and opened the note from Max.

Had to take a phone call. Will be back soon—M.

"Short and sweet," she said and folded the note away. She would have tucked it into her elegant evening bag, but before she could, someone snatched it from her.

"Ah, love notes," Elizabeth purred as she slid into the

booth with Janine. "I wonder what the happy bride-groom has to say…."

"Back off, Lizzie." Janine grabbed for the note, but the other woman held it out of reach.

When she'd read it, she turned a sympathetic glance on Janine. But her smile was pure mean as she handed the note back. "Such passion. I wonder now the paper didn't simply erupt into flames."

"Funny."

"No, dear. Quite sad, actually." Elizabeth held up a finger for a waiter and when he scuttled up, said only, "Vodka. Your best. Chilled."

Janine just looked at her. "Well, please. Sit down. Get comfy."

"I believe I will." Elizabeth crossed her legs with a slide of silk, stretched one arm out along the back of the deep red leather booth and said, "You and I should really talk, you know. We could be friends."

"Oh, I don't think so."

"But we share so much."

"Such as?" Where was her damn drink? Janine scowled into the crowd of partiers and wished fiercely that she were one of them.

"Max, of course."

"We don't share Max, Lizzie." Janine speared her with one long look. "I have him. You don't."

Score one for me, she thought, enjoying the flash of fury in Elizabeth's eyes. For the last three days, every time Janine turned around, there she was. Elizabeth took every opportunity to try to drape herself across

Max and, at the same time, edge Janine right out of the picture.

So far, she hadn't had much luck.

"It's Elizabeth," she said, her mouth barely moving. "And I have to wonder if you do indeed 'have' Max, as you put it."

Janine waved her left hand, letting the candlelight flash off the thick gold band she was actually getting used to wearing on her ring finger. "This says I do."

Of course, the ring lied, too, but Lizzie didn't have to know that.

Elizabeth sniffed dismissively. "That tacky little band says *temporary* to me."

"Tacky?" Janine glared at the woman, glanced at her ring, and then focused on the blonde across from her again. "It's not tacky. It's beautiful."

"And if you look closely, you can almost see the tiny, baby diamonds," Elizabeth said, not bothering to hide a sneer. "Now, the ring Max bought *me* was a five-carat yellow diamond solitaire. *That* was a ring."

"Sure," Janine said, rolling her eyes, "if you're trying to signal ships at sea. Talk about tacky."

"It was elegant."

"And showy."

"Beautiful."

"Vulgar."

"Why you little—"

The waiter showed up, carrying a tray with both drinks. Janine smiled a thank-you while Lizzie barely registered his existence.

Blowing out a long, infuriated breath, Elizabeth smiled grimly and inclined her head. "We'll leave the discussion of the ring for now."

"Why don't we leave *all* of it?" Janine shook her head and said, "Max'll be back in a minute or two. Do you really want him to see you here…*again*…looking all pitiful and doe-eyed? Where's your dignity?"

"My dignity is not at issue," Elizabeth informed her and took a sip of her iced vodka. "My future happiness *is*."

"Give it a rest, Lizzie. He doesn't want you. He wants me. And hey, look at the ring again. He's *got* me."

"For now, perhaps. But I think you and I both know that what you have with Max won't last."

If she only knew, Janine thought. Sure, the marriage was temporary, but that didn't mean that Janine was going to lie down so Lizzie could walk across her forehead. No way. She'd agreed to this little bargain with Max and she was going to do everything she could to hold up her end of it.

No matter *how* annoying it got.

"And I suppose you're the expert on lasting relationships?" Janine taunted. "No, wait. You're the *ex*-wife. I'm the new wife."

"Or current wife," Elizabeth said, "which is probably closer to the truth."

"What's your point? Even if Max and I split up in a year, we're together *now,* which should be plain enough even for you to understand."

"Unfortunately, you're not together, dear. Not in any possible sense of the word."

The band kicked it up a notch and the colored lights flashing on the dance floor seemed to pulse a little brighter.

"What's that supposed to mean?"

Elizabeth sipped at her vodka and leaned in over the table. Candlelight flickered in her pale blue eyes and it was like watching a spotlight dance across ice. "Of course, being a man, Max is blinded by your...charms. For the moment. But you can't possibly believe you're capable of being the kind of wife Max needs."

"And you were?" Janine snorted, despite the thread of irritation unwinding inside her. "I don't think he appreciated you dangling your lover under his nose."

"A miscalculation," she admitted. "But at least I knew how to be his wife. Have you ever entertained heads of state, dear? Pulled together a dinner party for a hundred?"

Janine squirmed a little, took a sip of her icy drink and told herself none of this mattered. She wasn't really Max's wife, so she didn't have to be any of the things Elizabeth was so enjoying pointing out that she wasn't.

"Hey, I do parties. I'll learn," she said stubbornly.

"I'm sure. With time and effort, you might even one day become adequate. But I wonder if Max will wait that long."

"Max wants me, Lizzie. Not you. Get over yourself."

Her features tightened, but she didn't quit. "Now, certainly. But once you've proven to him that you're nothing at all like the kind of wife he needs, I wonder if he'll still want you?"

"The point is he still *won't* want you," Janine said and watched that barb hit home. So, this little match could be considered a draw. Sure, she'd been stung at a few of Lizzie's taunts, but she'd had the last laugh.

Finishing off her vodka, Elizabeth fluffed at her blond hair until it swung loose around her shoulders like a golden cloud. "You're a fool, dear. A poor, simple fool. Max can hang all the diamonds he likes on you. But you'll never be worthy of them. And I think you know that as well as I do."

Janine took a gulp of her margarita. "Did you know you've got something green stuck in your front teeth?"

Elizabeth whipped her head back, ran her tongue over her teeth and then practically hissed at Janine. "Very amusing."

"Thanks, I thought so." Feeling better already, she took another sip of her drink and looked at the wide doorway to the club. Max was there. Looking gorgeous in black slacks and a white shirt, open at the collar. His black hair swept back from his forehead and his dark eyes stared directly across the room at her.

She felt the slam of heat rock through her and smiled to herself. Temporary or not, there was a very real connection between her and Max. Even as she looked at him, she could see his eyes darken from across the room.

"There's Max, now." Gathering up her bag, Janine scooted out of the booth, eager to get some distance between herself and the rabid dog Max used to be married to.

"Yes, run along like a good little peasant." Elizabeth nodded, then sighed suddenly. "My goodness. Who is that man coming in the door behind Max?"

"Watch it, Lizzie," Janine whispered, "your adoration of Max is slipping."

"Silly girl. Admiration of a handsome face costs me nothing."

Shaking her head, Janine stared across the room, smiled at Max, then shifted a curious glance at the man just now striding into the club. Tall, he had wavy blond hair, dark blue eyes and the tan of a perpetual beach lover. She knew his walk. Knew the confident air he wore as he cruised the crowd.

John Prentiss, one-time lover, full-time thief, walked into Fantasies and ruined what was left of Janine's vacation.

Seven

Janine actually took a half step toward John before she caught herself and stopped dead. Her instinct was shrieking at her to race up to that cheating snake and shake him like a cheap piggy bank until the money he'd stolen from her fell out. But she couldn't.

Not with Elizabeth standing right beside her.

The tall blonde was practically quivering with interest as she watched John stroll through the club like a great white shark in a school of guppies. But why should that surprise her, Janine thought. She herself hadn't seen John for what he was. Why would Elizabeth?

Nope. Janine couldn't afford to meet John here and now. She was supposed to be Max's wife. Which meant she couldn't be chasing down some other man while Elizabeth watched and plotted.

Damn it. She'd never thought she'd see John again. What kind of weird twist of fate was it to have him walk in when she couldn't confront him? Fine. She couldn't talk to him now. But that didn't mean she wouldn't face him down the minute she could shake loose of Max and his ex-wife.

Turning away quickly, so John wouldn't get a glimpse of her, Janine slipped through the crowd, leaving both Elizabeth and John far behind her. When she reached Max's side, she nodded and would have kept going, but his hand on her arm stopped her cold.

"Where are you going?"

She avoided looking into his eyes. "Outside. Need some air."

"Awfully sudden, this need for night air, isn't it?"

"Yeah, well..." She shrugged, forced a bright smile and said, "I'm a spontaneous kind of person."

His hand on her arm gentled, his thumb stroking her skin as if to soothe. "It's Elizabeth, isn't it?"

"No, it's not."

He clearly didn't believe her as he turned a frown on the woman across the room from him. "She's a stubborn thing when she's made up her mind about something."

"Oh, she's a pain in the behind all right," Janine said, pitching her voice to carry across the music and the low rumble of conversation behind her. "But Lizzie's not scaring me off. Don't worry about that."

"Glad to hear it. But if she's not worrying you, then what is?"

She pulled her arm free of his grasp, took a breath and turned around to look at the room she'd just crossed like an Olympic sprinter. Pointing as discreetly as possible, she aimed her index finger at John as he oozed up to the bar and zeroed in on a curvy redhead. "Him," she said. "My problem is him."

Max followed her gaze. "Did he say something to you?"

Janine smiled slightly in spite of the situation. The difference in men, she mused. John used women and Max instinctively moved to defend. Even his "temporary" wife. "No. In fact, he didn't even see me."

"Then…"

"That's John Prentiss," she said, watching her former fiancé turn on the charm. Sighing, she noted that the redhead was leaning in toward him now, smiling up into eyes that would be full of fascination. Janine remembered just how mesmerizing the man could be. How special he could make her feel just by giving her his complete attention.

And she hoped for the woman's sake that the redhead had her money under lock and key.

"*The* fiancé?" Max asked, interest in his voice.

"The very one." Janine turned her back on the crowd, looked up at Max and said, "So if you don't mind, I think I'm going to disappear before he spots me."

"Probably best," he said, "all things considered."

She turned to go again, but once more, Max stopped her with a hand at her shoulder.

"Max, come on," she said, irritation spiking. "I don't want him to see me and you shouldn't, either. Especially with Elizabeth out there, antennae quivering."

"Fine. We'll both go." He laid his right arm around her shoulders and steered her out of the club and down the wide tiled hall toward the lobby.

The music followed them. Candlelight glimmered on every table in the lobby, giving the room a flickering warmth that dazzled every bit as much as the fabulous views did during the day. And when Janine would have headed for the elevators, Max instead turned to the front doors.

"We'll take a walk."

She wasn't in the mood, but it wasn't worth arguing about, either. So she walked beside him and saw their reflection in the glass doors as they approached. They looked well together, she thought. Anyone on the outside would think that Mr. and Mrs. Max Striver were a handsome couple.

Which only went to show how wrong it would be to judge anything on appearances only. The doors slid open automatically and the cool ocean wind greeted them as they turned to walk across the grass, headed for the beach. The air smelled of flowers and the sea. The whispered hush of the ocean reached for them and above the sky was scattershot with stars that looked brighter here, somehow, than they did at home in the city.

And with every step, Janine felt her tension melt

away. Max didn't speak and she was grateful. After all, what was there to say? But the strength of his arm around her shoulder eased her stress level down several notches.

She stepped out of her heels at the edge of the sand and walked barefoot away from Max and onto a beach that still held the warmth of the sun. The wind here was sharper, colder and she welcomed the sting of it. Turning to look at the man still standing on the grassy verge, she said, "Thanks. Guess I really did need the air."

He tucked his hands into his pants pockets and studied her for a long moment before saying, "What do you plan to do about your fiancé's arrival?"

"I'd like to shove him back on a plane. Or better yet, underwater."

"Yes, I'm sure. However, it would be best if you simply avoided him."

She'd thought of that already, in the last few frenzied moments while her brain raced and her heart thumped hard in her chest. "It's a small island, Max. Going to be hard not to run into him."

"Will he believe you're married to me?"

"I don't know. Maybe." How could she possibly know what John would or would not believe? Clearly, she didn't know him as well as she'd thought she had. Or she would have spotted the whole "thief" thing in time to save herself.

"This is unfortunate."

She snapped a look at him. "Don't go all British on me, Max."

"That can hardly be helped," he pointed out, calm reason in the face of her rising fury.

God. What were the odds of John Prentiss showing up here? Was fate just playing with her mind? Or was this her chance to get back at the man who'd cost her so much? Was she being offered an opportunity here?

Or just another disaster?

"If he doesn't believe we're married, he could upset this situation before Elizabeth is convinced."

"I know that, Max." She dropped her heels into the sand, reached up and shoved both hands through her hair. "Why do you think I wanted to get out of the club so fast? But at the same time, I'm asking myself why I should have to be the one to avoid him. I'm not the thief. I'm not the one who did the lying and stealing."

Even in the moonlight, it was easy to see his features tighten and his brows lower over narrowed eyes. "Confronting him wouldn't gain you anything. Thieves don't usually make a habit of returning their spoils."

"I know that but—"

"And, you're in the process of earning back the money he stole from you."

"Yeah, but—"

"Do you really want to risk losing it all again for the momentary pleasure of facing him down?"

"Shouldn't I?" Janine took a step toward him and stopped. "He didn't just steal from me, Max. He lied to me. He—" She broke off and left what she might have said drift away. No way was she going to admit that John had broken her heart.

Fine, her heart had mended. She hadn't been emotionally shattered. She'd bounced back. But it had been a hard climb, pulling herself up out of the pit John had left her in. It wasn't just about the money. It wasn't even only about the lies.

It was, mainly, that he'd made her feel like a fool.

And damn it, she resented that most of all.

"Your motivation isn't in question," Max said, his voice low enough that she barely heard it over the pounding of her own heart. "What you have to consider is this. Do you really want this man to be the cause of more loss for you? Do you risk ending our bargain simply for the satisfaction of looking him in the eye and telling him you know what he is?"

She inhaled sharply, drawing the cold air into her lungs. She wished she knew what she was going to do, but she simply didn't. She couldn't promise *not* to talk to John. Sooner or later, they would run into each other—Fantasies just wasn't that big. But what she'd say when that time came?

She had no idea.

The following afternoon, Janine sat down beside Debbie's poolside chaise and listened to her friend's fury.

"He's *here?*"

"Yes, he's here."

"I can't believe it," Debbie said, whipping her head around, staring at the people crowding the area as if she could spot John Prentiss in the mix and fry him with a glare. "That lying, cheating, no good…"

Janine lifted her head, looked at her friend and grinned. God, it made everything better when you had someone ready to go to bat for you. Someone who understood, completely, how it felt to be made a fool of. To be lied to.

"Thanks, Deb."

"For what? I haven't found him and kicked his butt for you. Yet."

"No, but you want to and that's good enough for me."

Debbie swung her short, tanned legs off the chaise and reached out one hand to cover Janine's. "Where'd you see him?"

"In the club last night. Cruising the room, looking for his next victim, no doubt."

"What'd you say to him?"

"I didn't." Janine sighed, glanced over at the beautiful people splashing in the pool with enough care that no one's hair got wet. "I sneaked out before he saw me."

"You sneaked out? For God's sake, why?"

Looking back at her friend, Janine shrugged. "I couldn't talk to him. Elizabeth was there. And I'm supposed to be married to Max. Remember?"

Debbie drew her head back and stared at her as if she were nuts. "So because you've got a new man, you're not supposed to care about the lying, cheating snake who stole from you? On what planet does that make sense?"

"This one, as far as Max is concerned." Janine propped her elbows on her knees and her chin on her fists. "We talked last night. I told him John was here and Max doesn't want me talking to him. He thinks the creep will figure out that we're just pretending to be married and tip off Elizabeth."

"Oh, very nice."

"Can't really blame him," Janine said, though in a way, she did. He should understand, she'd told herself all night. She'd wanted him to be as angry for her as Debbie was. Which was unreasonable, she knew. After all, he didn't know her that well. He hadn't been around when John was taking her for a ride. Hadn't any personal interest in the fact that Janine's life had been shaken right down to the ground.

"So you're not going to say anything?"

"I didn't say that," Janine admitted. Max practically ordering her to avoid John didn't really sit well with her. After all, she'd done the good "wife" thing. Played by his rules. But this was important to *her* and he should know it.

She'd never be able to live with herself later if she didn't confront John when she had the chance. He'd stolen more from her than her money. He'd chipped away at her belief in herself. That wasn't something she could accept. Wasn't willing to accept.

And Max didn't even have to know about this. She could meet John, say what needed saying and then slip right back into being Mrs. Striver with no one the wiser.

Leaning in closer to Debbie, she whispered, "I have to. I have to at least stare him down and call him a thief to his face. I'd like to make him pay back every dime he stole from me, but even if all the satisfaction I get is telling him what I think of him, then that's what I have to do."

"Atta girl."

"I knew you'd get it," Janine said, smiling. Then the smile faded as she bit down on her bottom lip. "Max won't, though."

Debbie shrugged. "Why does he even have to know?"

"God, this is why we're friends. That's just what I was thinking a second ago."

"Good." Debbie smiled grimly. "Besides. Do you really think if someone had cheated Max he wouldn't take care of it? He wouldn't want some closure?"

Thinking about the man she'd come to know over the last week, Janine shook her head. "Not a chance. He'd do whatever he had to do. And so will I."

There was no reason she had to tell him she was going to hunt John down like a dog. No reason for him to be concerned with any of this. She could take care of John and still keep up the pretense of her "marriage."

She just had to be careful.

"What is this nonsense I hear about you having a wife?"

Max rolled his eyes and listened to his father's quiet fury bristling over the phone. He should have been more prepared for this conversation but in truth, he hadn't thought Elizabeth would move so quickly to spread the word around. "It was very sudden, Father."

"Too sudden to inform me?"

"Actually," Max said smiling, "yes."

"Who is she? Who's her family? Elizabeth tells me she's a very common-looking woman."

"Elizabeth would," Max said and felt a whisper of anger for the woman he'd once convinced himself he loved. Janine didn't look common. She simply wasn't as elaborately made up and artificial as Elizabeth. "Not that it's any concern of hers. Or yours, for that matter."

"I'm your father—"

"Not my keeper." Max's voice was steel and his father must have noticed. Stalking to the bar at the far side of the room, Max poured himself a short glass of single-malt scotch and tossed the liquor back quickly.

There was a long pause while the older man struggled to control his own temper before he said, "True, and yet, I find myself wondering why you didn't bother to contact your family about this hasty marriage."

"Sudden, not hasty," Max corrected. He wouldn't explain his relationship with Janine to the old man any more than he had explained his divorce from Elizabeth. Max was willing to concede that he had a duty to get married, have children. But he would do it in his time. Not his father's. He'd made that mistake once, in surrendering to family pressure to marry Elizabeth. And look how badly that had turned out.

"Fine, fine," the older voice rumbled in Max's ear. "You've put Elizabeth in a difficult position though, son."

"She's done that to herself. With your help." Pacing the length of the room, he continued, "Why the bloody hell did you tell her where I'd gone?"

His father cleared his throat, hemmed and hawed a

moment or two, then said, "She seemed eager to mend fences, whatever they might be."

Translation: Elizabeth had badgered the old man, then had cried to *her* father until he had gone to Max's father and demanded he do something. Elizabeth wielded tears like a broadsword in the hand of an expert.

"The only thing Elizabeth is eager for is to get more money out of me," Max said. "She's not happy with the divorce. Or with her settlement."

"Ah, that's a woman for you," his father said on a short, sharp laugh. "Of course she's looking out for herself. Any woman would."

Janine didn't, Max thought. Oh, she'd agreed to their bargain, but every time he presented her with jewelry or more clothing, she protested. She wasn't interested in Max's bank balance. She wasn't actively trying to bleed him for more than they'd agreed on. In fact, she'd outright told him all she expected from him was their agreed-on deal.

"That's damned congenial of you to be so forgiving of Elizabeth's mercenary nature."

His father grumbled into the phone. "Most marriages have difficulties, you know. At least you and Elizabeth share a background. Interests in common."

"Yes," Max allowed with a tight grimace, "we both enjoyed my money."

"Your mother and I had an arranged marriage," his father reminded him hotly. "And it worked out well in the end."

True. But then his mother hadn't been the kind of woman to take lovers on the side. Still, not something Max wanted to admit to another man. Not even his father.

"My arranged marriage did not," was all he said.

"No. But perhaps if you tried again…"

The elder Striver hadn't built the family business into one of the biggest in the world by giving up easily. This wouldn't be the first or last time he and Max butted heads.

"I'm already married, Father. Not to Elizabeth."

"Yes, yes." A gruff sigh of impatience came loudly across the line. "As you say. Well. It is your life, after all. But I want to meet this wife of yours. Soon."

Well, meeting Janine wasn't likely, he thought. Not when she would be returning to her own life in just a couple of weeks. Of course, Max would have to tell his father the whole truth about his sudden "marriage" once he went back to London. No doubt the old man would have plenty to say on the subject, but Max didn't have to think about that now.

He drew a breath, fought down a rising tide of frustration and blurted a change of subject. "Have you heard anything from the shipyard? Is the cruise liner going to be finished with the refit soon enough for the season?"

"Ah well, that is why I called and yes, they say the ship will be finished in…"

Max followed the slanting rays of the sun across the floor to the French doors where white sheers danced in a soft ocean wind. And, while the old man nattered on about a coming negotiation with a competitor, Max wandered out of the suite to stand on the terrace.

The sun was hot, streaming down from a cloudless blue sky. That slight ocean wind ruffled his hair and eased back the sting of the heat. Out on the sea, boats with brightly colored sails darted across the ocean's surface. On the beach, couples strolled hand in hand while two or three surfers rode the rush of waves to shore.

Max set one hand on the iron railing and stared down at the pool area below him.

There was a crowd of people gathered around the infinity pool. Lush, flowering plants edged the tiled patio and the sound of laughter drifted on the air like music. It wasn't difficult to spot Janine talking with her friend. And as Max's gaze locked on his counterfeit wife, he began to think about everything he'd told his father about her.

He smiled when she laughed and then wondered if perhaps life wasn't handing him an opportunity.

His gaze moved over Janine and even from this distance, his body stirred. She attracted him like no one else ever had. And he actually liked her. She made him laugh. Didn't take herself, or him for that matter, too seriously.

Added to that, seeing her with Elizabeth over the last couple of days had only underlined the two women's differences. Where Elizabeth was cool sophistication, Janine was open, warm. In bed, Janine heated his body until he felt as though he were being swallowed by an inferno, and he'd never known anything close to that with anyone else.

Though they were only pretending a relationship, what he and Janine shared was far more real than anything he'd had with his ex-wife. In fact, Janine played her part of wife so well—in public as well as in private—that even Max was convinced that she actually cared for him.

All of which led him to consider the "opportunity" erupting in his mind. What if he suggested their arrangement become permanent? What if they were truly married?

While his father talked business, Max thought about his life. He and Janine got on well. As lovers, they were an excellent match. And, over the last couple of days, she'd shown that she could play the part of his wife with ease.

Why not make it legal? It would work for both of them. She wouldn't have to worry about financial difficulties—not to mention, there would be no reason for her to concern herself with John Prentiss any longer. And Max would have a marriage and one day, a family—without having to add emotions into the mix.

"Are you paying attention?" his father demanded.

Max smiled. "Of course." But as the old man continued with his one-sided conversation, Max turned his mind instead to possibilities.

Eight

A few days later, Janine was still looking for her chance to approach John Prentiss.

She had to be alone to do it and as if he knew just what she was waiting for, Max made sure she was never alone. As if he were attached to her side, he was always there, insisting that as "newlyweds" they should spend as much time together as possible.

Not that she minded his company—God knew, she was really enjoying this time with him. More than she had thought she would. This faux marriage of theirs was getting easier to pull off, too. They were actually becoming a couple, which was something Janine hadn't counted on. Sure, she'd gone into this arrangement with her eyes wide open. But she hadn't thought she'd come to care for Max so much. Hadn't thought that she'd get so used to having him with her during the day—and beside her at night—that the thought of never seeing him again would tear at her so.

"You'll survive," she whispered, as if saying the words aloud would make her believe. And of course she'd survive losing Max. What they had wasn't real. She knew that.

She just wished it didn't *feel* real.

And, she thought with a sigh, added to everything else going on in her world, Lizzie was never far away. The woman couldn't seem to take a hint. And she showed no signs of surrendering gracefully to Max's new "wife."

Sitting under a red-and-white striped umbrella on the poolside patio, Janine took a sip of her iced tea. "Speak of the pain in the rear and in she walks," she muttered as she watched her "husband" and his ex-wife thread their way through the crowd to join her.

Another typically beautiful day at Fantasies, there were at least a hundred people scattered around the patio, having lunch or a drink, or simply enjoying the setting. As Janine had been, up until she'd spotted her elegantly dressed nemesis closing in on her.

Even from a distance, she could see Max's frustration and Lizzie's determination. The woman was practically sprinting trying to keep up with Max's long strides and while she ran beside him, she never stopped talking. Though she couldn't hear her, Janine would have been willing to bet that Lizzie was delivering yet another tirade on how unsuitable Max's new wife was and how much better off he'd be if only he went back to Lizzie.

"What kind of woman," she wondered aloud, "works so hard to get the attention of a man who clearly isn't interested?"

Was it the challenge? Maybe. But in Lizzie's case, Janine was willing to bet it was ego run amok.

Lizzie simply was *not* the kind of woman men walked away from. At least, she didn't think so.

Max gave Janine a tight smile as he walked up to the table and stopped beside her. His eyes rolled as Lizzie rushed up behind him. Ignoring her, he quipped, "Lovely day."

"For some of us," Janine said, letting her gaze slide to Lizzie.

The woman's hair was mussed, and a sheen of dainty perspiration shone on her face. Not a good idea to run in the sun if you were trying to maintain the aura of perfection.

"Gee, Lizzie," she said, "you look all worn out. Would you like some iced tea?"

The other woman sneered at her, took a deep breath and then ran one hand over her hair, tucking the few escaped strands back into formation. "Thank you, no. Max and I were having a private conversation, if you don't mind, so why don't you…" She waved a hand to indicate that Janine could take herself off anywhere at all and Lizzie would be happy.

"We were not having a discussion at all," Max said,

placing a kiss on Janine's forehead and taking the seat beside her.

"And even if you were," Janine pointed out with a smile, "it didn't look private. Not with the way you were doing the Olympic sprint and shouting after Max."

Max smiled and Elizabeth went into frosty mode.

"I do not shout."

"If you say so," Janine said and had to admit, if only to herself, that she was sort of beginning to enjoy these little sparring matches with Lizzie. And she wondered what that said about her.

"Max," Elizabeth said, ignoring Janine entirely now, "I think it would be best if you and I spoke privately."

"I'm sure you do," he said and dropped one arm around Janine's shoulder. "But I need a moment alone with my wife, so I'm sorry to say I'm unavailable to you."

The sleek blonde was still struggling to catch her breath but she managed to huff out a spare burst of air. "Really, Max. Your wife can do without you for a moment."

"Wow. First time you've said the word *wife* without a sneer," Janine said. "Kudos."

Now the sneer appeared.

"There it is after all."

"Isn't there somewhere else you need to be?" Elizabeth urged.

"Hey," Janine pointed out with a lazy wave of her hand, "I was here first. You came to me."

"I didn't come to you—I was following—er, I came with Max."

"Elizabeth," Max interrupted. "If you don't mind…?"

"And even if you do?" Janine smiled.

Straightening up, Elizabeth lifted her chin, fingered the strand of pearls at her throat then managed a smile that only partially resembled a grimace. "As you wish. But Max, I do need to speak with you. Perhaps tonight. Dinner?"

"That's sweet of you to ask, Lizzie," Janine said, completely ignoring the fact that *she* hadn't been included in the invitation. "But Max and I will be having dinner alone. In our suite."

"How very cozy for you both."

"Yes, isn't it?"

"Perhaps tomorrow then." Elizabeth smiled at Max, glared at Janine, then slunk elegantly away, moving through the crowd like a benevolent queen through a throng of ungrateful peasants.

"You're getting very good at handling her," Max said.

A cool wind off the sea ruffled Janine's hair and teased the fabric of the umbrella she sat under into a quick dance.

"It's not that hard, really. I treat her like I would a spoiled three-year-old. Plus, she gives me all the openings I need." She picked up her iced tea, took a sip, then offered it to Max.

He took a quick drink then frowned. "Why don't you use sugar?"

"And spoil the taste of the tea?" she countered. "Just what kind of British guy are you?"

"The kind," he said, leaning in closer and teasing the ends of her hair with his fingertips, "who has to attend a business meeting in Florida tonight."

A swirl of something she was afraid to admit might be disappointment surged through her and Janine quickly battled it down. If she was going to miss the man for a few hours, how would she ever do without him once they returned to their own lives?

Stirring the tea with her straw, she listened to the soft click of ice cubes hitting crystal before she said, "How long will you be gone?"

"Only overnight." He leaned back in his chair now, shifted his gaze over the crowd briefly and then looked back to her. "I couldn't get out of it. One of our accounts needs to see me about some plans for expansion."

"Sounds important."

"It is." He stretched out his long legs, crossed his feet at the ankles and studied her. "If it weren't, I wouldn't go."

"Well then," she said, forcing a smile. "What time's your flight leave?"

He grinned at her and Janine felt a straight shot of something sizzling rush through her. The man really could get to her as nobody else ever had. Probably not a good thing, she decided, since this whole relationship was so temporary. How in the hell would she ever be able to date some average Joe at home without mentally comparing him to Max?

And how would any man ever be able to measure up?

"*My* plane is gassed up and ready to go whenever I arrive at the airfield."

Of course it was. How foolish of her to have forgotten even for a minute that Max ruled his own little world. A world where flight schedules meant nothing because he could call up his own jet on a moment's notice. A world Janine had no place in.

"Right. Wasn't thinking. So, when do you leave?"

"Now." He straightened up in his chair, rested his forearms on his thighs and leaned in toward her. "I just wanted to see you before I left. Make sure you'd be all right dealing with Elizabeth on your own."

"Please." Janine laughed, set her tea down and reached over to lay one hand on his. "Lizzie doesn't worry me."

He nodded, frowned, then asked, "And you'll stay away from Prentiss, as we discussed."

It wasn't a question. It was a simple statement of fact. Which was exactly why it irritated her.

"Max..." She sighed, lifted her hand from his and only sighed again when he caught it and held it trapped between his palms. Staring at him, she said, "Let it go, okay? What's between John and I is none of your business."

"It is now that we've got our own bargain running, Janine. And I won't have it spoiled by a petty need for revenge."

"Petty?" Now she yanked her hand free of his grasp and tried to remember why, only moments ago, she'd been sorry to hear he was leaving. "It's not petty. He lied to me. Used me. Stole from me. If someone did that to the great Max Striver, no way would the guy just walk away unscathed."

He glanced around as if to assure himself that no one

was paying attention to them. Then, when he looked back at her, his eyes were narrowed and his voice was low and tight. "Whatever he did to you, it's over now. You survived it. Let it go and move on."

She shook her head at him and knew he would never understand. Irritation warred with disappointment, and disappointment won. "Wow. You should put that on a T-shirt. Great advice, Max."

His voice was low and somehow more British with the sting of banked temper in it. "You're making this more difficult than it is."

"I'm not making it anything. You're the one with the bug up the wazoo about it."

"The—never mind," he said. "I don't want to know."

She sat back in her chair, folded her arms over her chest and tapped the toe of her ridiculously expensive leather sandals against the tile. "Just as well."

"As I thought," he said. "You're being very short-sighted about this, you know."

"Oh, am I? And how's that?"

"You're so interested in confronting this man, you've forgotten that you're already beating him." When she frowned at him, he kept talking before she could interrupt. "He thought to leave you broken and bleeding. He thought to ruin you. To shatter your life. But he didn't."

"Damn right he didn't," Janine said, remembering though, how she'd cried, how she'd mourned and how she'd felt the fool once she'd understood that John'd slipped out of town with all of her money.

He reached out again, grabbed the sides of her chair and turned her around so that she was facing him squarely. She didn't want to look into his dark eyes. Didn't want to feel anything but the anger churning within.

"You hung on," Max said. "That took guts. And now, you've found a way to earn back what he took from you. You can go home now and rebuild your life into exactly what it was before he entered it."

Logical. Completely logical. She knew that.

But she didn't care.

She wanted to look into John's lying eyes and tell him she knew him now for what he was. She wanted to demand her money back because she knew that was the only way she'd earn back her self respect. But she couldn't tell Max any of that because he didn't know. Could never know how it felt to have your heart torn out of your chest and tossed at your feet.

So she kept her thoughts to herself and let him talk.

"But if you face him now, you lose everything. You prove that you are the foolish woman he thought you to be." His gaze was dark, and steady. "Is that what you want?"

"No," Janine said tightly and shifted her gaze from his. "I don't appreciate you talking to me like I'm a child, either, by the way."

"You're not a child, Janine," he whispered, going down on one knee and leaning into her. He turned her face with the tips of his fingers until she was looking into his eyes again. "You're a woman with a sharp, clever mind. A woman who is, I believe, too smart by half to make the same mistake twice. Don't let John ruin you again. Don't give him the satisfaction."

"You're pretty clever yourself," she said, trying to ignore the tiny pinpoints of heat his fingertips engendered on her flesh. "Turning this all around to put it on me. Did you take psychology in college or something?"

He grinned fiercely. "Or something."

"Fine," she said. "Don't worry about me. I'll be a good little wifey. I'll stay away from John and I'll try to keep from punching Lizzie dead in the face."

"Much appreciated," he said, laughing.

"But don't expect me to think about this the way you do, Max." She pulled her head back, stared at him and said, "I can't. I won't."

He sighed and his brow turned into a frown. "You're a stubborn woman. I believe I may have mentioned that before."

"A time or two."

Nodding, he stood up, rested one hand on her shoulder, then bent down to kiss her.

His mouth moved on hers and despite the anger churning within, Janine couldn't help but be moved. It was her damn body's fault. Everything in her lit up for Max like a fireworks show on the Fourth of July. Her blood sizzled, her heartbeat pounded and her brain went a little fuzzy as his lips and tongue teased her.

Finally, he pulled his head back, smiled at her and said, "I'll try to hurry through the meeting."

"No rush," she quipped, but damned if she didn't

hope he came back fast. Not fair to heat her up only to leave town.

He grinned, as if he knew exactly what she was thinking. "Take care."

She watched him walk away and noticed that several other women were watching him, too. Well, she thought, why wouldn't they? All they saw was a tall, amazing-looking man with a great behind. They didn't know how pushy and bossy and overbearing he was to live with.

They didn't know that the man understood *nothing* about women. They didn't know that he'd just given her a direct *order* for Pete's sake.

And they, like Max, had no way of knowing that she had no intention of following his order.

Later that night, Janine was ready. She wore yellow capris, a white shirt and brown sandals. She wasn't dressed like Mrs. Striver. No diamonds. No silks. To face John, she wanted to do it as herself.

Besides, if John got a look at some of the jewelry Max had given her, he'd find a way to steal it.

Walking out the hotel's glass front doors, she fought down the nerves battling to take over. Her stomach churned and her blood raced. She'd seen John heading for the beach just a half hour ago. If she moved fast, she could catch him, hopefully alone, and say what she had to say with Max never being the wiser.

Her steps were quick, light as she moved through the darkness. Her heartbeat was pounding, her stomach still spinning but her course was set. She'd waited too long for this chance to pass it up now. Janine crossed the lawn, continued down the slow slope of grass to the edge of the sand. Once there, she stepped out of her sandals and carried them as she walked toward the water.

He was there. Watching the sea, as if he knew exactly the kind of picture he painted. A gorgeous man on a starlit beach, waiting for a lover.

Or, in this case, a furious ex-lover.

"John."

He turned, saw her and just for an instant, cool deliberation flickered across his face. Then a moment later, his expression eased and a practiced smile curved his mouth. "Janine. I didn't expect to speak to you again."

His voice rippled through her and she remembered so much she didn't want to recall. The way he'd whispered to her in the night. The first time he'd told her he loved her. The night he'd proposed.

Then she remembered his all-too-brief goodbye note—and the empty echo inside her savings account. Pain was still there and that surprised her. But it was quickly drowned by her simmering anger. "I bet you didn't."

"What're you doing here?" He turned his back on the ocean to face her, tucked his hands into his pockets and kept that smile in place.

"I'm on vacation," she said, walking closer.

"Oh, I knew that," he told her. "I've seen you a couple of times with your *husband*."

She swallowed hard. The emphasis on the word *husband* told her he knew something—or thought he did.

"I didn't come to talk to you about Max," she said. "I want the money you stole from me."

"Janine," he said, his voice holding a note of disapproval. "You *wanted* to give me that money. An investment."

"Uh-huh. And how's it going, my investment?" Her nerves were gone and in their place was a cool detachment. God, how could she have ever believed him? How could she have looked at him, loved him, and not seen the truth of him? "How about some dividends?"

"There've been some setbacks," he admitted with a shrug. "Unfortunate downturns."

"Right." She lifted both hands to encompass the resort, the fact that he was there and hey, probably on her money. "Looks like you've had some setbacks, all right."

"Investing is risky."

"For some more than others. Look, John, I'm here to tell you that you'd better find that investment for me."

He pulled his hands free of his pockets and held them out helplessly. "Sorry, babe. No can do."

She'd expected that. Known he'd fight her. And was prepared.

"If you don't," she said, moving closer, "I'll tell everyone on this island just what you are. A thief. A liar. A man who romances a woman until he can steal everything she's got. Be a lot harder to find the next woman to fleece."

His eyes narrowed. "I wouldn't do that."

"Really. Why's that?"

He grinned again and even managed a short, amused laugh. "Well, *Mrs.* Striver, I figure you've got a few secrets of your own to keep quiet."

Janine rocked backward on her heels. He knew. How? A cold wind whipped off the ocean, making her eyes tear.

"You're the talk of the resort, babe," he was saying. "The whirlwind romance of a nobody and the very important Max Striver. Congrats, by the way."

Fury choked her, held a tight fist around the base of her throat and made even breathing difficult.

He didn't wait for her to say anything; he just kept talking. "See, I know you, Jan. You don't do anything without a plan. There is no way you would have been swept off your feet by anybody. Unless you married him for his money, in which case, what makes you better than me?"

"You—"

"So, I figure this puts us at a stalemate, Jan honey."

"Don't call me that."

His grin widened. "You say anything about me, I'll blow the whistle on you."

"There's nothing for you to tell."

"Oh, come on. A man like him? Marries someone like you in an overnight romance? I don't think so. There's something there. I don't even have to know what it is, though if you want to tell me, I'm all ears." He paused. "No? That's okay. Like I said, I don't have to know. All I have to do is start the wheel spinning. Gossip. Rumor. A few whispered questions and people will talk. Speculate. It'll ruin whatever it is you've got going and you know it."

He was right. Gossip didn't need facts. Rumors didn't have to be based in reality. He could ruin her again if she allowed it. Then she'd be right where Max had said she would. Nowhere.

"You're a real bastard, aren't you?"

"Sticks and stones," he said, clearly enjoying himself now.

Before she could even think about it, she charged. Swung her hand back to slap his face and he grabbed her wrist with one lightning-quick move, Yanking her up close to him, he looked down into her eyes and said quietly, "You back off, I back off, Jan honey. We go our separate ways and call it a draw."

Pressed up against him, she felt as though her skin was crawling. How had she ever cared about this man? How had she made love to him and not seen what he really was? And how had she thought, even for a minute, that she'd be able to outwit him? John made his living by lying and cheating. She was only an amateur.

"Let me go."

"We have a deal, then?"

"Yes," she blurted, disgusted with him and with herself. God, she should have listened to Max. Should have stayed away from John. Because now, she'd allowed him to make a fool of her twice.

"Glad to hear it," he said and let her go. Smiling con-genially, he suggested, "Now you really should be going. I'm expecting someone any moment."

"Your next victim?"

"That's a little harsh."

She choked out a laugh that felt as though it were torn from her throat. "Fine. I'll go. Hell, she probably wouldn't believe the truth about you even if I told her. Poor woman."

"As I recall, you didn't have any complaints."

"Maybe not then. I've got plenty now." She was furious. And humiliated. And disgusted. More with herself than him. She'd walked into another mess with her eyes wide open. She'd allowed John to win. Again. Damn it.

"Then you should probably hurry on back to your 'husband.'" His gaze left hers, looked past her, and that smile she remembered so well touched his face. "My date's arrived, so I really think our time together is over, Jan."

She glanced over her shoulder and saw Lizzie mincing her way across the sand on impossibly high heels. For God's sake. This just kept getting better and better.

"Janine?" Elizabeth said when she was close enough. "If you've decided to start taking a lover already, you might take one who's not already spoken for."

"Trust me on this, he's all yours."

She turned to hike back up to the hotel, grimacing tightly as she heard Lizzie's delighted laughter floating

on the air behind her. Just perfect. She'd been humiliated by both John *and* Lizzie.

Could this night *get* any worse?

Nine

Max saw it all.

He'd rushed through his meeting in Miami and flown back earlier than expected to surprise Janine. As it turned out, he was the one surprised.

He watched, hands fisted at his sides, as Janine met with John Prentiss in the moonlight. He was too far away to hear what was said, but fury choked him when the tall blond man grabbed Janine and held her pinned to him. Jealousy spiked inside him, an emotion he was unfamiliar with—one he'd never experienced before. But the jealousy was nothing compared to the urge to rescue Janine from the man handling her so roughly.

Before he could rush to her aid though, she tore herself free and in another moment or two, she turned from the man just as Elizabeth strode clumsily across the sand toward them.

While one corner of his mind noted that his ex-wife was suddenly focused on a man other than himself, Max was too fixated on Janine to enjoy Elizabeth's distraction.

His gaze caught and locked on the woman who was his temporary wife. A dizzying mix of emotions churned inside him, and he fought to sort them through. Fought to maintain the icy calm for which he was known. But even as he grasped at the slippery ends of his control, he muttered, "Why the bloody hell did she meet with the man directly after I expressly told her not to? What was she thinking? Damned woman never listens."

When Janine started back over the sand, heading quickly toward the resort, Max stepped out of the shadows. He watched her face, saw the anger glittering in her eyes, saw the pinched look to her mouth and could practically feel the fury radiating off her in thick, hot waves.

Until she saw him.

Then she stopped dead, glanced guiltily over her shoulder at the beach she'd just left and took a long, deep breath before shifting her gaze back to his. "Max. I thought you were in Florida."

"I was." Betrayal chewed at his insides. He knew the feeling well. Remembered it all too clearly. And now, here he was again. Once more, his woman was out meeting another man. Perhaps Janine hadn't made vows, but she had made a promise. And perhaps the reasons were different, but the sting of deception was just as sharp. Somehow, he'd expected better of Janine and that made this all the more irritating. He'd actually considered making her his *real* wife. He'd come to think rather highly of her only to find she was, in effect, no better than Elizabeth.

The wind ruffled her short brown hair, tossing the unruly curls into a waving, dark halo. She scraped her palms over her hips, then folded her arms defensively across her chest. "I didn't know you were coming back so soon."

"Yes." He bit the word off, hardly trusting himself to speak. "I can see that."

"Fine. You're pissed." Her arms dropped to her sides, then she reached up to shove both hands through her hair with impatience. "Go ahead and say it."

"Where shall I begin?" He silently congratulated himself on keeping his voice level and his fury tamped down. "I told you to stay away from him."

Now her restless hands moved to her hips. "I don't take orders from you, Max."

He bristled. "Clearly."

"I had to see him."

A couple strolled out the front doors of the hotel, their whispered conversation and laughter somehow making Max even more angry.

"Bloody hell, Janine." He stepped toward her, grabbed her upper arm in a firm grip and practically dragged her away from prying eyes, farther into a moonlit garden. The grass was damp, the flowering shrubs flavoring the air with a tropical sweetness.

But the beauty of the place was lost on him. Anger pumped through his body and Max felt himself nearing the ragged edge of restraint. Deliberately, he let her go, took a step away, and then turned to look at her. "You've risked a lot," he told her. "By meeting with another man, you've put everything in jeopardy. Was it worth it?" he wondered aloud. "Did you find satisfaction? Did he promise to repay you?"

"No," she said and began to wander the enclosed garden. She walked to a hibiscus plant and gingerly ran her fingers over a soft pink flower. She didn't look at him as she continued. "No to all of it. There was no satisfaction. It wasn't worth it and of course he won't pay the money back."

Stuffing his hands into the pockets of his slacks, Max gritted his teeth. "You knew that. You knew bloody well he wouldn't before you ever faced him and yet, you simply couldn't help yourself. Why? Why when you're in the position of earning back what he stole, why was it so damned important to demand restitution from him?"

At last, she turned her head to look at him. In the moonlight, her complexion looked softly bronzed. Her dark eyes flashed and the mouth he usually found so tempting firmed into a grim line. "Because it wasn't just about the money, Max. That's what you don't get."

"Of course I get it," he snapped, unwilling to traipse back over the same blasted argument they'd had the last time they'd discussed her former fiancé. "We've been over this."

"But you don't understand." She stalked toward him and stopped directly in front of him. "He took something from me you can't compensate me for."

He huffed out a breath, shook his head and pinned her with a dark gaze. Janine met that stony stare with one of her own. Fine. She felt guilty. She shouldn't have met with John. She felt terrible that Max had caught her red-handed while breaking her promise to him. But damned if she'd feel *badly* about facing John. It was simply something she'd had to do. She only wished she could make Max understand.

"This wasn't about the money," she said and willed him to listen. To really hear her. "This was about what he did to *me*." She slapped one hand to her chest and felt the thudding of her own heart beneath her palm. "He took my sense of self from me. He stole that as surely as he did the money. He took away my pride. He scampered off with my belief in myself. And that's something our little bargain won't earn back for me, Max. I had to find it on my own."

A silent, tension-filled moment passed before he asked, "And did you? Did you find what you needed?"

"Truthfully? I don't know." Janine lifted her chin and kept her gaze fixed on his. "I feel better for having looked him in the eye and told him what I think of him. I feel less used, somehow. Less a victim."

"And I'm supposed to applaud now, I suppose? Say

well done, Janine? I'm expected to commend you for breaking your word to me. For going behind my back?"

"I don't want your applause, Max," Janine said, suddenly tired as adrenaline drained away, leaving her a little shaky. Why was she bothering to explain herself? Clearly, all Max was concerned with was the bargain they'd made and how her confrontation with John would affect it. And still, she said, "I would like you to at least try to understand."

"Yes. I expect you would." Then he turned around, walked into the hotel and left her, standing alone in the moonlight.

"Well, forget him," Debbie said the next day as she and Janine walked on the beach. "I mean seriously, what an ass. How could he *not* understand about you needing to face down John the Jerk?"

"Thanks, pal," Janine said and bent to pick up a broken seashell tossed ashore by the blue-green waves. She ran her thumb across the ridged surface, then turned and threw it back into the water.

The rush of foam-topped waves continued relentlessly toward shore and the wet sand beneath their feet sank with every step. Seagulls whirled in a noisy dance overhead and several surfers sat on their boards, waiting for their next ride. Farther out to sea, sailboats skimmed the water's surface, sails bellied out in the wind. Janine squinted into the brilliant sunlight to focus on the beauty around her. Anything really, to help take her mind off her own problems.

"He didn't even come to bed last night," she said softly. "Max?"

"Of course Max, who else?"

"Well, sounds like he was really pissed. And you should have been, too," Debbie pointed out. "Did you really *want* him in bed with you?"

The answer to that question should have been a resounding *no*. But it wasn't and Janine knew it. She *had* wanted him with her. She'd wanted his arms around her. Wanted his body moving into hers. Wanted him to whisper in her ear that he did understand. That she'd done the right thing.

Ha!

And she might as well have wanted to be crowned Queen of the Known Universe.

"Oh," Debbie said, then winced. "Ouch. So you still wanted him even though he acted like a supreme idiot."

"Yeah. So what's that say about me?"

Debbie shrugged, threaded her arm through the crook of Janine's and said, "It says you like him. A lot. Even when he's an idiot."

Janine snorted. "Well hell. If we only liked men when they *weren't* idiots—"

"Good point." Debbie grinned and shook her long blond hair back from her face. "So. What're you gonna do about it?"

"Why should I have to be the one doing anything about it?"

"Because, as you just pointed out…men…idiots."

"He's seriously pissed, Deb."

"And you care?"

Janine just looked at her friend.

"You *do* care. How much?"

"Too much."

"Hell, honey. Why'd you have to go and fall in love with him?"

"I didn't say *love*—" She stopped herself, took a breath and blew it out again. Who was she kidding? This had been coming on since she'd first met Max. She'd known the danger going in and she'd risked it by putting herself in the position of pretending that what they had together was real. And now, she'd gone and made the dumbest move of her life. "Fine. Okay. I do love him. So who's the real idiot here?"

"Still him," Deb told her and gave her a nudge with her shoulder.

"Thanks." Janine stopped, looked back at the resort behind them, standing on a knoll like a castle. And inside that castle was her very own prince. The only problem was he didn't know he was the prince. And he wouldn't care that she loved him.

Lousy fairy tales.

"What in the hell am I going to do?"

"What you always do," Debbie told her. "Lead with your heart, no matter what happens."

"Yeah, and that worked out so well the last time."

"Sure. But John was a JERK, capital letters, and Max is just an idiot. There's hope."

Janine laughed, and felt better than she had since Max had left her alone in the darkness. God, what would she do without her friends? Didn't even want to think about it. But was Debbie right? Was there really any hope where Max was concerned? He'd made it plain going in that he was only interested in a temporary setup. Love had never been mentioned and she had the distinct feeling he wouldn't like it mentioned now, either.

Besides, he didn't trust her.

She'd seen his eyes clearly enough last night to see past the anger and identify the mistrust glittering there like glass shards.

And she had no idea how to get past that.

The main bar at Fantasies was on the lobby level. A wide open space, it was filled with glass tables dotted with small ruby vases boasting tiny white flowers. Sunlight was muted through the tinted glass walls that surrounded the room, providing a view of the grounds, the beach and the ocean.

Max, though, wasn't noticing the ambience. Instead, he kept his gaze fixed on his untouched glass of thirty-year-old scotch. His fingers idly played with the crystal tumbler, moving it in slow concentric circles on the table. His mind couldn't settle any more than his hands could.

He kept thinking about Janine. About the talk they'd had the night before and how he'd walked away from her. Well bloody hell, what else did she expect? he wondered, silently fuming. She'd gone behind his back. Betrayed him. Was he supposed to then turn about and be the understanding male?

Not bloody likely.

He was still furious and, in keeping with that feeling, had continued to avoid Janine. He'd slept in the second bedroom of the suite—and didn't want to admit even to himself that he'd slept badly because she hadn't been there—and he'd left the suite as early as possible, to elude her again. No doubt, like every other female he'd ever known, she would want to "talk" about what had happened.

Well, they'd talked enough, he told himself. And he wasn't nearly ready to let go of the fury crouched inside like a snapping beast.

"You look like you're ready to break something."

Irritated, Max looked up, then smiled at his old friend. "Gabe. Don't worry. Your crockery's safe."

"Glad to hear it." Gabe sat down opposite him, signaled a waiter for some coffee, then leaned back in his chair. "So. What'd you want to see me about?"

Max had almost forgotten about calling Gabe and asking him to meet him in the bar. But now that the man was here, he found himself hesitant to say what he'd come to say. Still and all, who better to ask. "You have a guest here. John Prentiss."

"All right." Gabe took his coffee from the waiter, nodded his thanks and then lifted the cup for a sip.

"What do you know about him?" Max asked the question knowing that Gabe was the kind of man who made it his business to know whom his customers were. To hear if there were complaints.

"Offhand? Not much." Gabe shrugged, set the cup

down and said, "Seems to be popular with the ladies. Plays a lot of high-stakes poker in the casino every night. What else do you need to know?"

"No grumbling or grievances about him from anyone?"

"Not yet." Gabe's features tightened perceptibly. "Should I be keeping an eye on him?"

Max thought about what he knew of John Prentiss. What Janine had told him. He had only her word and the information he had gathered from her background check. But… "It might be wise."

"I'll look into it," Gabe said as he stood up and walked off.

Thoughtful now, Max remembered the look on Janine's face the night before. When he'd left her, so wrapped up in his own sense of annoyance that he hadn't wanted to admit even to himself just how damned…regal she'd looked in the moonlight. But now he couldn't stop thinking about it. And about what she'd said. And perhaps she was right. Perhaps he couldn't understand what her former lover had done to her.

Disgusted now, he lifted his gaze to take in the bar area. Doing a quick scan of the room, he spotted John Prentiss at a table and instantly made up his mind to talk to the man. He wanted to see for himself if the man was everything Janine insisted he was. Standing, he carried his drink with him to John's table. "Mind if I join you?"

The blond man looked up, seemed to take him in at a glance and then said, "Sure. Be my guest."

"Thanks." Max sat down and watched as John

tucked away the newspaper he'd been reading. "John Prentiss, isn't it?"

"That's right. And you'd be Max Striver."

"I would. I wondered if we might talk."

"About Jan?"

Why hearing the other man call Janine by an intimate-sounding nickname should strike him so wrong was beyond him, but Max shut those feelings down and cut right to the heart of the matter. "My wife tells me you took advantage of her."

John smiled winningly, spread both hands out as if in supplication and shook his head slowly. "Now, that's simply not true."

"Really?" Max took a sip of his drink, then set the glass aside. Folding his hands on the glass table, he cocked his head, studied his adversary and said, "Why don't you tell me what really happened, then?"

John leaned back in his seat. Lacing his fingers together loosely atop his abdomen, he said, "I hesitate to spread stories about another man's 'wife.'"

Catching the emphasis on that last word, Max lifted one eyebrow, stared hard into the man's clear, watery blue eyes and encouraged him. "I'm sure it's distasteful to all of us. And yet…"

"Fine then." John nodded, sat up and lowered his voice into a tone of sympathetic regret. "I'm sorry to say that your wife once tried to blackmail me into marriage."

"Is that so?" Something tightened inside him, but Max kept his features carefully blank. He was known in the business world for his poker face and it stood him in good stead.

"Oh, yes." John nodded, lifted his martini glass and took a sip. Setting it down again, he stared directly into Max's eyes and said, "When I tried to end our relationship, I'm afraid Janine became hysterical. Why, she even pretended to be pregnant—in a blatant attempt to get me to marry her. Told her friends we *were* engaged. Sad, really."

"Yes, I'm sure." Max's mind raced while the other man talked. Janine? Hysterical? Those two words didn't seem to fit well together. Though granted he'd only known her a little more than two weeks, he'd seen enough of her moods to know that hysteria wasn't one of them.

"Fortunately, I found out at the last moment that she wasn't pregnant." John smiled and shook his head again, as if sorry for the poor, pitiful woman who'd tried to cheat him. Max didn't know whether to believe him or punch him.

Yet…a small corner of his mind wondered. While John continued talking, Max asked himself if any of this could possibly be true. Though he didn't like the look of Prentiss—the man had a weak chin and a gaze that continually shifted to one side—Max had to admit that he was wondering about Janine. Asking himself what the real story was. Yes, he'd investigated her and she seemed to be all she claimed to be. But even seeing proof on paper wasn't enough to completely convince him to trust Janine. Once burned, it seemed, forever shy.

He wanted to trust her. But the truth at the bottom of it all was that he didn't.

After all, why would a woman who was willing to take money to pretend to be married, hesitate to lie her way into a real marriage?

Still, his instincts told him to be wary. Both of Janine—and the man she had once been in love with.

"I spoke to John today."

"What? Why?" Janine turned on him in the bedroom of the suite they were sharing.

"I wanted to see what he had to say for himself," Max told her and adjusted the fit of his black suit coat. Catching her eye in the mirror, he said, "After all, I'd only heard your side of the story."

"My side. That's great. Thanks for your support." Janine bent down, grabbed a red silk high heel and shoved it onto her right foot. Balanced on that slender heel, she used her left foot to turn the matching shoe over before stepping into it.

Turning his back on the mirror, he faced her, shoving both hands into his slacks' pockets, idly jingling the change. "Aren't you curious as to what he had to say?"

Yes.

"No," she snapped and grabbed her red clutch purse. She couldn't believe they were going down to dinner together. He was still furious with her and she was still sure there was no reaching past the mistrust hanging between them. And yet, Max insisted they continue their charade. Appear at the crowded rooftop restaurant and behave as any other "happily married couple."

How was she supposed to act *happy?*

"He tells quite the different story," Max said.

"Not surprising," Janine muttered, fluffing her hair with one hand and walking to the mirror to check her makeup one more time. "He'd hardly admit to you that he's a thief and a liar."

"On the contrary. He says you tried to blackmail him into marriage by pretending a pregnancy."

"He *what?*" She turned around to look at him so quickly, her heel caught on the throw rug and she was forced to grab hold of the dresser to stay upright. Fury, rich and hot, raced through her. She felt the heat of it on her skin, in her blood. And when she looked up into Max's eyes, she wanted to shriek. "You *believed* him?"

A very long moment passed before he said, "No."

"Gee. Feel the warmth."

"Wear the rubies tonight," Max told her blandly.

"Wear the—I don't care about jewelry and how can you when you're telling me something like this?"

He reached past her, flipped open the lid of the jewelry box atop the dresser. Snatching up long gold-and-ruby drop earrings, he passed them to her.

They felt cold in her hand.

God. She felt cold. The fury was gone, replaced by an emptiness she had the feeling would never completely leave her. How had this all turned out so badly?

"You know what, Max, I can't do this anymore." She dropped the earrings onto the dresser and shifted her gaze from his. "I can't pretend to be your wife. Can't play at your game and make it believable. Not when you think so little of me. Not when I know that you think I'm capable of—God."

He laid both hands on her shoulders and waited until she looked at him again. "You're not backing out of this now, Janine," he said tightly and his eyes were unreadable. "You'll play the part you've chosen to play. And when Elizabeth leaves Fantasies, I'll pay you what we agreed upon and then you can go home. Back to your flower shop. Find your next rich fool."

His words slapped at her. "You said you didn't believe him."

"That doesn't mean I believe *you*." He handed her the earrings again. "Now finish getting ready. We have reservations."

Ten

The next few days limped past.

Janine felt more alone than she ever had, despite sharing a bed every night with a man she loved.

Max was cool, withdrawn. There was no snuggling in the dark. No reaching for her to pull her close to his hard, warm body. There was polite chitchat instead of laughter and hard feelings on both sides instead of the "we're in this together" attitude they'd shared at the beginning of this little adventure.

And Janine was pretty pissed off about the whole situation.

"This is just wrong," she complained for what had to be the tenth time in as many minutes. "I'm the one who did *nothing* wrong and I'm being made to look like a money-grubbing fortune hunter or something!"

"Well," Debbie said from the pool chaise beside Janine, "you *did* go to meet with John right after Max asked you not to."

"*Told* me not to," Janine corrected, then practically snarled, "and whose side are you on, anyway?"

"Yours!" Debbie held up both hands in surrender. "Totally. Your side. Completely."

"Okay, then." Janine sat up, grabbed her water bottle and took a long drink. Her head was pounding and her stomach was doing a weird spinny thing. She drew in a deep breath and ignored the off feeling. "Deb, he looks at me like I'm trying to pick his pocket or something."

"Then why are you staying?"

Someone in the pool screamed in delight and droplets of splashed water landed around her like fat raindrops from a bright blue sky.

"Huh?" She picked at the label on her water bottle with her thumb.

"I said, why stay?" Debbie sighed, swung her legs off the edge of the chaise and sat up. "Cait'll be back from Portugal any time now. And she's already told you she'd get Lyon to loan you the money that Max is going to pay you. So why stay when you're obviously miserable?"

Good point. She'd asked herself the same question several times over the last few days. And she only came up with one answer. Because she'd given her word. And she wouldn't break it again.

The truth was she *had* broken a promise when she'd gone to meet John. Sure, Max had ordered her not to go, but she'd agreed, then gone right ahead and done what she'd wanted anyway. Look how well that had gone. So she wouldn't break her word again. She'd stay because she'd promised him she would. Because she wasn't going to give him another reason to think she was a liar.

"No." She took another drink of her water and gritted her teeth. "I said I'd stay and I'll stay. I gave my word on it, Deb. Only a few days left anyway. And you know what? I *earned* that money from Max and damned if he's going to get out of paying it."

"Man, you're stubborn."

"Yeah, guess I am." She screwed the lid back onto the empty water bottle and set it aside on a nearby table. "One upside to this is Lizzie's spending so much time with John lately, she's leaving me and Max the hell alone."

"Well now," Debbie mused, "John and Lizzie. There's a match made in hell. I guess Karma's alive and well and Lizzie's going to get what's coming to her."

"Yeah." Janine frowned and shifted her gaze to the crowded pool where tanned, hard bodies frolicked in warm water. "I admit, a part of me's thinking, *Good. Lizzie's getting what she should.* But there's another voice in my head telling me I should warn her about John."

"She wouldn't listen."

"Not the point, is it?" Janine looked at her friend again. "Shouldn't I tell her anyway? It's the right thing to do, isn't it?"

Debbie just stared at her for a second or two. "Both Lizzie and John have tried to screw with you and you *still* want to be the good girl?"

"It's a curse."

"I'll say." Debbie leaned in closer, lifted her sunglasses and peered hard at Janine. "You're awful pale. Are you feeling okay? You look sort of…off."

She swallowed hard. "Actually, I'm not feeling very well. My stomach's a little upset."

"Not surprising."

"I suppose." Blowing out a breath, Janine picked up her towel and stood up. "I think I'm going upstairs to lie down for a while. I'll catch up with you later, okay?"

"Sure, sweetie." Debbie stood up, hugged her quickly, then let her go again. "Go take a nap. Forget about Max for awhile."

It wasn't that easy, Janine thought as she headed inside. Because even when she slept, her dreams were filled with Max.

That night, Max dropped in on the casino. He didn't much care for gambling ordinarily, but then that night, he wasn't there for the games.

Taking a seat at a high crystalline bar, Max ordered a drink and watched the crowd. Elegantly dressed people moved in and out of the table games, laughed and shouted at the slot machines, and over it all, rock music flowed from overhead speakers. The lights in the casino flashed and dazzled and winked off the diamonds worn by the women wandering the packed floor.

From his seat, he had a view of the high-stakes poker room, and Max focused his attention on one of the players. John Prentiss, wearing a well-tailored tuxedo, held court at one of the tables. Even from a distance, Max could see that the man bet wildly. Extravagantly. His manner was exuberant, over-the-top, and Max wondered how a woman like Janine could ever have thought herself in love with such a clearly shallow individual.

Why would she try to "trap" this fool into a marriage?

And as he wondered, he had to ask himself if any of what John had told him was true. Max took a drink of his scotch, set the glass down onto the bar and wondered if he'd been entirely fair to Janine. Or had he been susceptible to John's side of the story because of his own experiences with a woman's betrayal?

"He's up tonight."

Max turned to look at Gabe as his friend walked over to join him.

"Prentiss, you mean?"

"Yeah." Gabe leaned one elbow on the bar, shook his head at the bartender, silently telling him he didn't want a drink. Nodding in John's direction, Gabe said quietly, "He plays fast and hard. Last couple of nights, he's had some heavy losses, but looks like his luck turned tonight."

"Do you always pay such close attention to your guests' gambling records?"

Gabe lifted one eyebrow and smiled. "Nope. I only watch the ones I hear talk about."

"And people are talking about Prentiss?"

"Oh, yeah." Gabe turned his back on the crowd, braced his elbows on the bar top and turned his head to look at Max. "I've had three different people tell me about some 'investment' opportunities Prentiss is offering."

"Is that right?" Max's voice was thoughtful, his gaze piercing as he stared at the man raking in stacks of chips.

"Uh-huh. One of my regulars said it sounded shifty to him, but a couple of others are interested." He swung around now to face the poker table again. Keeping his voice low enough to be barely heard over the clattering noise of the casino, he said, "I'm keeping an eye on him. I don't allow thieves to make their next mark in my place."

"Thief? There's proof?" Max ground his teeth together and thought about how he'd been treating Janine the last few days. He'd allowed John Prentiss to sway his opinion of her and for that he wanted to kick his own butt.

"Not much. But there's talk. And when you run a place like this," Gabe said, a proud smile flashing across his face, "it pays to listen."

"Good policy," Max mused, remembering now that he himself had checked into John Prentiss before he'd ever offered Janine the bargain she'd agreed to. He'd discovered then that the man had disappeared with her money. And yet, even knowing that, he'd been prepared to believe John's practiced lies over Janine's furious indignation.

What kind of man did that make him?

Had he really become so distrusting that even when faced with truth, he would rather believe a lie?

"Isn't that your ex?"

Following the direction of Gabe's gaze, Max saw Elizabeth enter the casino like a goddess awaiting worshippers. She stood in the entrance, wearing a column of white silk that kissed the floor at her feet. Her hair was twisted into an elaborate knot on top of her head and her features were cool, detached, as she looked about the room.

"Yes. That's her." Max saw the flash of delight in her eyes when she spotted John Prentiss and he knew that his fondest wish had come true. Elizabeth had finally shifted her attention to someone else.

They had nothing but bad blood between them now, and yet, he briefly considered going to her. Warning Elizabeth about John Prentiss—even knowing she would never believe him.

Then that decision was taken from him.

"Well, this can't be good." Gabe's voice broke into Max's thoughts, and he saw Janine walk into the casino and stop alongside Elizabeth.

Janine wore red. Red-hot enough to inflame him even at a distance. Her one-shouldered gown sleeked along her curvy body like a song. Her short dark hair looked casually tousled, and her features, as she addressed Elizabeth, looked strained.

"Why is she deliberately talking to her?" Max wondered aloud even as he stood up and prepared to cross the room in as few steps as possible to reach the women.

"Are you nuts?" Gabe grabbed Max's forearm to

hold him in place. "Any man who purposely gets into the middle of that is certifiable."

Max was forced to agree as he watched the two women begin what appeared to be a heated exchange.

"Leave me alone," Elizabeth said in a command filled with her usual venom.

Janine wouldn't be ignored, though. She'd decided only an hour ago to talk to the other woman. Warn her about John. Whether or not Lizzie deserved a warning didn't come into it. Janine couldn't simply stand by and watch another woman be victimized by an expert.

"Look, Lizzie," she said, keeping her voice low enough to be nearly swallowed by the clatter and rush of the casino, "I'm trying to do you a favor, here."

"Ah yes," the other woman said with a short laugh. "Because we're such chums. Of course you'd want to help me in any way possible."

"Fine. I hate you. You hate me. This isn't about us."

"Rest assured," Elizabeth said, her eyes narrowed dangerously, "I'm no longer interested in Max, so we don't have that to discuss, either."

"I didn't come to talk about Max."

"Then what could we possibly have to say to each other?" She moved to step past her, but Janine was quicker and blocked her path. *"What?"*

"It's about John Prentiss." Janine took a quick breath, ignored the flash of anger in the other woman's eyes and kept talking. "He's not what he seems to be. He's a thief and a liar and if you're not careful, he'll take you for as much as he can before he dumps you on the side of the road."

A long sizzling minute passed before Elizabeth snorted in disgust. "This is pitiful."

"I'm sorry?"

"As you should be." Elizabeth lifted her chin and looked down her patrician nose in a manner that told Janine the woman had been learning that particular move since she was a child. "John told me what you might say about him."

"John—"

"He told me exactly what kind of woman you are," Elizabeth said, leaning in now, so her voice could be a whisper of sound and still be heard. "Trying to trap him into a marriage with the threat of a false pregnancy. I knew the first time I saw you that you were beneath contempt. This only proves me right."

Janine felt a flush of heat and fury race to fill her cheeks and only hoped that Lizzie wouldn't think it was embarrassment. "For God's sake, of course he'd tell you lies about me. Do you think he'd be *honest* about setting you up?"

"Pitiful." Elizabeth shook her head and gave Janine a dismissive glance. "I find you to be completely pitiful and frankly I don't know what Max saw in you in the first place. But if my ex-husband was foolish enough to be ensnared where John would not be, then shame on him."

"Lizzie, you don't understand...."

"On the contrary, I understand completely," the other woman said with a sniff of distaste. "You couldn't trap

John and now you're trying to see to it that no one else will find the happiness with him that you were denied. It's all quite simple, really."

Janine felt a swell of regret. She wasn't going to be able to get through to Lizzie. Why had she even tried? Stupid really to think the woman would believe her about anything.

"Fine." Janine nodded, swallowed hard and said, "You've made up your mind. I wish you luck with him. You're going to need it, Lizzie."

"If I were you," Elizabeth told her, "I would be more concerned with my own welfare than that of others. I assure you, I have no compunctions against telling anyone who will listen just exactly what type of woman Max has married. Whatever you think you've gained will be smeared with your own unsavory reputation."

Janine took a breath but before she could speak, the other woman cut her off neatly.

"John and I will be leaving, going to my home in London the day after tomorrow. Until then, I would appreciate it if you could refrain from being in my presence."

"No problem," Janine muttered as Elizabeth sailed past her and walked smiling toward the man who would, eventually, break her heart as well as her bank account.

Well, Max would be pleased. He wouldn't have to worry about Lizzie hunting him down like a trophy anymore. Just two days, she thought as John smiled at Elizabeth and drew up a chair for her to join him. Two more days and this bargain would be over. She could go home. Reclaim her life. Go back to the flower shop and work to forget everything that had happened on the vacation she'd wanted so much.

Max walked out onto the dimly lit patio and slipped up behind Janine quietly. She stood at the stone railing that edged the terrace and looked out at the black sea, glittering in the starlight. Her chin was lifted, her eyes focused on the horizon and her hands were curled tightly over the balustrade.

"You tried to warn her, didn't you?"

She didn't jolt at his surprise intrusion, merely turned her head and looked at him, as if she'd been expecting him to appear. "Yes."

"She wouldn't listen."

"No." Janine lifted one hand to smooth her hair back from her forehead, and the diamond bracelet he'd given her flashed in the light. "John's much more convincing than I am. You should know that."

Max winced a little. "I suppose I deserved that."

"Yeah, you really did."

He stepped closer, turned his back on the sea and leaned one hip against the stone railing. The cold damp soaked through the fabric of his tuxedo, but he hardly felt it. He looked into her eyes and saw so many things. Regret, disappointment, anger, all churning together. And he knew he owed her something.

"I don't say this very often," he said quietly as her gaze fixed on him, "but I owe you an apology."

Her eyebrows lifted into delicate arches above her fathomless eyes. "About…?"

"You know very well about what," he said and reached out for one of her hands. Taking it between his, he felt the chill in her skin and wondered if it was from the air or what she was feeling. And he wondered how much of what she was feeling could be blamed on him. "I was wrong. About you. About Prentiss. About many things."

"Wow." She smiled all too briefly then shifted her gaze back to the ocean stretching out before them. The music from the casino was softer here, more muted, but there was enough to fill the silence building between them. "This is a moment we're having."

Now it was Max's turn to smile. He should have expected that apologizing wouldn't be enough. He'd hurt her. And that actually had never been his intention. Now, he was hoping that he might both win back her trust and do something that would benefit each of them.

He pulled her close, opened his thighs and held her, trapped between them, pressed tightly to him. "Janine, I'm telling you I believe you. More, I believe *in* you."

"That's nice, Max, but…"

"I understand that I behaved badly."

"Ah yes. Calling me a cheat and insinuating that I was willing to trap some poor rich man into marrying me. Yes, that was behaving badly, wasn't it?"

"*Very* badly," he amended and was pleased to see a tiny flash of humor spark in her eyes. "It was good of you to try to warn Elizabeth."

She frowned. "No woman deserves to be had like that."

"She'll make her own choices," he said, knowing

that Elizabeth had already charted her course. She'd decided to have John Prentiss and no one would be able to talk her out of it. And who knew? Perhaps they might even be happy together. After all, Elizabeth was a wealthy woman in her own right—she'd only wanted to add to her coffers by marrying Max. Perhaps John Prentiss would actually be satisfied with this woman and her money. "You couldn't dissuade her no matter what."

"No, I guess not. I didn't really expect to," she admitted, laying both hands on his shoulders. "But I had to try."

"And I respect you for that effort."

A soft wind caressed them, the sweet scent of tropical flowers floating on the air.

"Thanks."

"So I'm forgiven then?" His hands at her waist tightened, his fingers sliding over the silky red fabric of the dress he wanted to get her out of as soon as possible.

"Why not?" Janine shrugged, cupped his face in her palm and said, "You were just being you, Max."

He chuckled wryly. "I don't know whether to be pleased or insulted by that."

"Always good to leave 'em guessing," she quipped, then stepped out of his embrace and smiled. "You should know, Lizzie and John are leaving the day after tomorrow."

Max nodded and stood up to face her. This then was as good a time as any to tell her of his proposition. With Elizabeth gone, their bargain was almost at an end.

"I'd like you to think about something," he said,

then scowled when a clearly drunk couple staggered out of the casino and onto the terrace. Taking Janine's arm, he steered her around the edge of the balustrade and out onto the grassy area where they could be more private.

Here, the scents of the sea and the flowers surrounded them. The shadows hid them. And he used both as he drew her into his arms and looked down into her eyes.

"Max?"

"Janine, our time together is almost over," he began, letting his gaze move over her features. "And I think you'll agree that but for a couple of bumps in the road, we've done well together."

"Yeeesss…" She dragged that one word out into several wary syllables.

"I'd like you to think of extending our bargain."

"What?"

"No, not so much extending as redesigning."

"What're you talking about, Max?"

"It's very simple, really," he said, bending his head to plant a quick, hard kiss to her delectable mouth. "I think we should be married legally. The two of us get on well. We're very compatible, both in bed and out. It's perfect, really."

Her mouth fell open.

He rushed on. "You can have your own flower shop if you like, when we get to London."

"How nice for me."

Max frowned a little, but kept going. He wanted to get it all said. "Janine, we've both been badly burned at relationships based on so-called 'love.' This would be far better. We can both enjoy a marriage, children, a *family,* without risking emotional damage."

"You're serious, aren't you?"

"Never more so." He grinned now, staring down at her surprised expression, convinced that he was doing the right thing. For both of them. Surely she would see that. "What do you say?"

Eleven

Janine looked up at Max, noting the pleased expression on his face. Clearly he was delighted with himself and his clever proposal. He was also damned sure of himself. He had the air of a man who knew he was about to get what he wanted.

Too bad he was about to get shot down instead.

Hurt warred with wounded pride and anger, and surprisingly, the hurt won out. Her heart felt as if it had taken a hard slap and the sting of tears burned at her eyes. But damned if she'd cry for him. So she blinked the sensation away and shook her head.

"Sorry, Max. I won't be the bought-and-paid-for bride for you."

"I beg your pardon?"

She inhaled sharply, blew out a breath and watched as consternation, and then anger flitted over his face. "You're trying to buy a real wife, just the way you bought a pretend one. I'm not interested."

"I'm not trying to bleeding *buy* you for God's sake," he snapped.

"So the flower shop just for me isn't the bribe? It's the reward?"

He sighed heavily, like a man forced to endure far more than any man should. Shoving both hands into his pockets, he grumbled, "I only meant that you could do the work you love in London as easily as you could in Long Beach, California."

Another twinge of pain rippled through her, sending ribbons of misery to every corner of her body. Strange. She shouldn't be so wounded. She'd known full well that Max didn't have feelings for her. It wasn't his fault she'd fallen in love and ruined their perfect little deal.

But pain made her a bit less than understanding, she supposed.

"I'm not interested in a faux life, Max," she said with a slow shake of her head. "Three weeks of pretense is one thing. A lifetime is quite another."

"It wouldn't be a faux life, Janine. It would be *our* life."

"As long as nothing messy like real emotion, real depth of feeling gets involved?"

He scowled at her. "Bloody hell, woman. Haven't you already been down that road?"

"Yes," she said, taking another deep breath of the

floral air, "but I went down that road alone. I'd like to have someone with me the next time."

"I'm not interested in love, Janine."

"That's a shame, Max," she said. "For both of us. Because I love you."

His eyes narrowed and his jaw muscle twitched. She could only imagine he was grinding his teeth together hard enough to turn them into dust. "You don't."

Janine actually laughed, though the sound was harsh and it felt as though her chest was tightening around her shattering heart. "I probably shouldn't love you, it's true," she said. "God knows it would be a lot easier if I didn't. But I do."

"For God's sake, why do all women have to bloody well confuse things with *love?*" He stalked away from her a few paces, stopped dead, then turned to look back at her. "I didn't ask to be loved. I don't want to be loved."

"With that attitude," she managed to say, "don't worry about it. You won't be loved by many."

"But you do," he said, disbelief clear in his tone.

"Clearly, I like the crabby type." She walked up to him, each step measured. Her gaze locked on his and she saw the regret shining in his eyes along with frustration. "If you think I wanted to feel anything for you, you're wrong," she said quietly. Laying one hand on his forearm, she felt his muscles bunch and tighten beneath the elegant tuxedo jacket. "I didn't expect to fall in love, Max. And I don't expect anything from you, now. I'm just saying, I won't marry you. Not like that. Not with no feeling. With nothing more than a signed contract between us."

He didn't speak, but then he didn't have to.

Janine dropped her hand from his arm and smiled sadly. "If I did that, I'd end up hating myself for loving someone who *refused* to love me. And I won't do that, Max. Not even for you."

By the following afternoon, Janine was wishing she were already home in Long Beach. She'd had enough of the rich and fabulous lifestyle, thanks very much. She needed to be back at work. Back living the kind of life she understood.

Back where she could start forgetting about Max.

"I can't believe you didn't slug him for that," Cait muttered, obviously disgusted. "I've known Max for years and I cannot believe he could make such a stupid proposal!"

"He's a man, Cait." Debbie shook her head and took a drink of her iced tea. "You've only forgotten that because you're still in the 'glow' of new love."

"Thank you oh, wise woman," Cait said, then shifted her gaze to Janine. "How'd he take it when you said no?"

Janine leaned back in her chair. She and her friends were having lunch on one of the resort's patio restaurants. It was good to have Cait back, and it was great to have them both supporting her in this. But the truth was she didn't want to talk about Max and his stupid proposal anymore. She just wanted to get through the next day or so and then go home.

"He wasn't happy," she said and stabbed at her tea with a straw.

"Typical," Debbie said, taking a bite of her penne pasta. "He doesn't see that *you're* unhappy?"

"I don't know." Janine pushed her chef's salad to one side, suddenly not up to even looking at the crumbled blue cheese on top, let alone smelling it.

"Well," Cait said, as if guessing that Janine simply didn't want to talk about any of this anymore, "Jeff and I are going home early. Tomorrow, in fact."

"What?" Debbie asked. "Why?"

"My mom," Cait admitted. "She's calling me two or three times every day now to talk about the wedding."

"Bet Lyon's loving that," Debbie said.

"He's being very sweet," Cait told her.

Janine stayed out of it. She listened to her friends and told herself she should join in. Get involved. Not think about Max. But the hurt she'd been wrapped in since the night before wouldn't ease long enough for her to see beyond it.

"I'm going to stay an extra week," Debbie said. "I'm enjoying being pampered. I called home last night and told Trudy she could call or fax me if there are any problems."

"Must be nice to own your own business," Cait said with a laugh.

"It has its perks." Debbie reached over and squeezed Janine's hand. "You still feeling yucky?"

"A little."

"You're sick?" Cait leaned in, too.

"No," Janine said softly, swallowing hard against a small wave of nausea. "Just a little…bleh."

All around them, happy people chatted. Silverware clinked against fine china, and waiters and waitresses bustled through the crowd, keeping everyone content.

"Uh-oh." Cait stared at her long and hard, until Janine finally shifted uneasily in her seat.

"What?"

"Um…" Cait shot Debbie a worried look. "How long have you been feeling 'bleh'?"

"Just the last few days and—" She broke off, looked from Cait to Debbie and back again before finally seeing the unsaid questions in their eyes. "No way."

"I didn't say anything," Cait blurted.

"You didn't have to. You think I'm…I can't even say it."

"You mean pregnant?" Debbie asked.

"Thanks. Saying it out loud won't jinx me or anything." Janine's hands dropped to her flat belly. "I can't be pregnant. It's too quick."

"Hmm… How long's it supposed to take, then?"

"You're not helping," Janine said, glaring at Debbie.

"Fine. Go find out. Buy a test. Flunk it."

Cait shrugged and gave her a small smile. "She's right. Take a test. Then you'll know."

"That's the trouble," Janine muttered.

Early the next morning, Max watched as Elizabeth and John left Fantasies together. A mountain of luggage accompanied the smiling couple as they walked out to the waiting limousine. And with his ex-wife officially out of his life, Max took a long, deep breath and enjoyed the heady sensation of freedom that surged through him like a rising tide.

If Elizabeth was walking blithely into disaster, there was no stopping her. And she, unlike Janine, was no longer his problem.

He still couldn't understand why Janine had turned down his offer of marriage. Especially if she really did "love" him as she had insisted. Wouldn't she be happier with him than without him? Wouldn't she rather be a part of his life than live on separate continents?

Was her love so miniscule that unless it was reciprocated it would wither and die?

Of course she wanted to marry him, he told himself with a hard nod. She simply wanted to be wooed. Convinced. And he could do that. Why, this was even better than he had thought it would be. If she actually loved him, then he would at least be able to count on the fact that she wouldn't be dangling lovers in front of his eyes.

He would be a good husband and father.

All he need do is ask her again.

Couch his exceptionally reasonable proposal in such terms as to make her see the clear benefits to her.

Smiling now, he started across the lobby for the elevator, sure he could make his temporary bride see reason.

"No way."

Janine looked at the white plastic stick in her hand

and shook it as if it were a Magic 8-ball and would give her a different answer. But nothing changed.

She was still pregnant.

Slapping one hand to her forehead, she leaned against the bathroom counter and stared into the mirror at the face of a woman who was well and truly screwed. Then a small thread of hope showed on her reflected face. "The pharmacist said it was too early. That I might get a messed-up answer. That's probably it. I'm probably not pregnant. The test is just messed up. Debbie was wrong."

She let her forehead rest on the cold glass of the mirror as that tiny hope drained away in the face of what she *felt* to be true.

"Not Debbie's fault. My fault. Well, and Max's. Oh man. One time? That one time we forgot a damn condom and this is what happens?"

She opened her eyes, looked at herself and sighed. How was she supposed to tell Max about this? Their agreement was at an end. They were about to go their separate ways. And now she had to tell him she was pregnant?

In the harsh glare of the bathroom lights, she shook her head at her image in the mirror. "He'll never believe me. Especially not after the story John told him. He'll think I'm lying about a baby to trick him into marriage."

No.

Wait.

Maybe not.

Her eyes lit up and another spark of hope fitfully

clung to life inside her. "He asked me to marry him already, right? If I was willing to trick him into marriage, I wouldn't have to. I could have just said yes when he asked." She nodded, smiled woefully and said, "So he'll know this isn't a trick. A lie. He'll believe me. He won't be happy, but he'll believe me."

She slumped down onto the closed toilet seat. "What if he doesn't believe me?"

"Janine?"

She jolted and threw a quick look at the closed bathroom door. "In here!"

"Ah. Fine. When you come out, we have to talk. Elizabeth just left with John."

Janine sighed. Well, she had enough to worry about. She couldn't spare another thought for the bear trap Lizzie was stepping into. The woman was on her own.

"Okay," she called back, and congratulated herself on the steadiness of her voice. "Be out in a sec."

Staring down at the pink plus sign in the middle of the plastic stick, she muffled a groan, then buried the stick at the bottom of the bathroom trash can. No point in Max seeing the damn thing until she'd had a chance to tell him about this herself.

When she came out of the bathroom, Max was waiting with a welcoming smile on his face. "Congratulations are in order to both of us," he said. "Elizabeth's gone and our bargain convinced her to move on."

"Yay us," Janine said and walked past him, through the bedroom into the plush living room. Taking a seat in one of the well-cushioned chairs, she curled her legs up and watched Max as he came into the room behind her. "So then, the deal's complete. Task finished."

"Yes," he said softly and held out a single sheet of paper to her.

She took it, her mind racing, and tried to concentrate on the three lines of typed print on the page. When she'd read it, she looked up at him. "You've already wired the money into my bank account?"

"As agreed." He took the chair opposite her, leaned forward and braced his forearms on his thighs.

"Thank you," she said and folded the paper neatly, closing her fingers around it. No matter what else happened now between she and Max, at least Janine knew that she wouldn't lose her home. She'd be able to take care of her baby—alone if she had to.

Her *baby*.

Oh, God. Her stomach shivered and spun. She was going to have a baby. Max's baby.

"Janine," he said, his voice soft and easy, "I've been thinking about our discussion in the garden last night."

"Me, too," she admitted.

"Brilliant," he said, clearly pleased.

Obviously he had convinced himself that she'd changed her mind. That she was more willing now to talk about entering into a loveless marriage.

"But, Max…"

"Now, usually I prefer to say ladies first. This time however, I want to tell you what I'm thinking before you say anything. All right?"

"Fine." She swallowed the knot of nervousness clogged in the middle of her throat and fought to focus solely on Max. On what he might say. There was still a chance that he was willing to try to love her, wasn't there? Shouldn't she hear him out at least? Besides, she was just coward enough to appreciate having a few more minutes before she had to tell him her news.

"I want you to reconsider," he said, smiling at her with all the warmth she'd come to know he was capable of. "We're bloody good together, Janine. There's no reason to throw that away for lack of emotion."

"Oh, Max…" Disappointment welled inside her and only swelled as he continued to talk.

"You say you love me," he said, gaze fixed on hers. "Well then why not marry me? If love is important to you, you already have it."

"But you don't love me," she pointed out.

"I…care for you," he admitted and it sounded as though he'd had to grab hold of the words and drag them from his own throat. "And I find I will miss you when our time together is finished. Isn't that enough? For now, at least?"

Oh God, she was tempted. Especially now. Especially knowing she was carrying his child. But how could she risk living with a man who might never love her? How could she tie herself forever to a man who had no *interest* in loving?

No. Not even for the sake of the child she carried would she live with the emptiness of knowing that she loved alone.

"No, Max. It's not enough."

He sat back in his seat and his features slipped from congenial to angry in the blink of an eye. "You're being ridiculously adolescent, Janine. You know that, don't you?"

"No, I don't." She stood up slowly and looked down at him. "I need to be loved, Max. I deserve to be loved. If you can't or won't do that, then we can't be together."

"Love is for children. For fools who trust their hearts more than their heads."

"God, I hope not," she said on a sigh. Then she inhaled sharply, looked at him and said what she had to say before leaving him forever. "I'm going to pack, Max. I'm leaving on the first flight out I can get."

"Janine—" He stood up, looked into her eyes.

"But before I go, there's something you have to know." He waited and in the deafening silence, she said, "I want you to know that I seriously considered not telling you this at all. But that wouldn't be right. And now that I'm talking, I'm feeling a little nervous about the whole thing so I'm just going to spit it out. Get it over with. Throw it out there so you'll know the whole truth."

"At which point will you be imparting this news?" he wondered.

He was right.

She was stalling.

"Fine. Here it is. I'm pregnant."

A heartbeat, then two, then three passed before he took a step back from her, looked her up and down and

snorted a harsh, disbelieving laugh. "This was unneces-
sary," he said tightly. "I'd already offered to marry you."

"This has nothing to do with—"

"Oh, of course not. It's simply a convenient twist of
fate that finds you pregnant with my child." He laughed
again, walked away from her as if he couldn't stand to
be in close proximity any longer, then turned and glared
at her. "The amusing part of all this is I believed you to
be innocent. I thought John had lied about you trying
to use an imaginary pregnancy to trap him into
marriage."

"Max," Janine said, fighting the insult, fighting the
hurt clamoring inside her, "I'm not lying."

"Damned if you're not quite good at this!" He
laughed again and the sound was like knives slashing
the air. "But you may as well realize, you won't be
getting any more money out of me than the sum we've
agreed on."

She swayed as if his words had been a physical blow.
This was what he thought of her? At the base of it, the
heart of it, he thought she was after his damned money?
She looked at him and knew that in his mind, he'd
lumped her alongside Elizabeth, and that not only hurt,
it made her furious.

"I'm not asking for anything from you."

"You've overplayed your hand, Janine," he said and
now his voice sounded weary. "I won't play this game.
And by the way? You might think of developing a new
routine. This stratagem is getting a bit frayed around the
edges, don't you think?"

Janine stared at him and saw the hard glint in his eyes and the defensive posture in his stance. There was no bend in Max Striver. He went where he pleased, ran his life as he liked and dismissed anyone who got too close.

Well, fine. She'd leave. But she wouldn't go without telling him exactly what she thought of him.

"You're an idiot, Max."

"I beg your pardon?"

"You really should," she started, squaring her shoulders and lifting her chin. "You know what's wrong with you?"

"I'm sure you're about to inform me," he said with idle disinterest.

"Damn straight. You've spent way too much time in the rarified atmosphere of the rich and useless, Max. You look at those of us who don't have billions and think we're all after your money. Well the hell with your money, Max. I don't want it and don't need it. I made a deal. I earned what you paid me, but that's all I'll ever ask of you.

"I pay my own way. Live my own life. I don't need billions to survive, unlike *some* people."

"If you're finished…"

"Not even close," she snapped. "You can't see the truth when it slaps you in the face, Max. You're always ready for a lie because you trust no one. Fine. Maybe Lizzie did treat you badly. Get over it already."

He furiously sucked in air. "If you think you can—"

"I've more than earned the right to tell you off, Max, so just shut up and listen." Sunlight speared through the

French doors and gilded him in a wash of light that made him look so handsome, so completely amazing that it nearly killed her not to go to him. But that time had passed. "You think you're the only one who got stepped on? Take a look around, Max. Lots of people have a lot harder life than you do. But you know what? They go on anyway. They trust again. They love again. They *live*."

His eyes were no more than black slits watching her. "Have you finished *now?*"

She blew out a breath, looked at him one last time and realized that nothing she'd said to him had gotten through. "Yep. I guess I have."

Several long, quick strides carried him across the floor to the door. He opened it, turned and looked back at her with an icy gaze that sent shivers rolling along her spine.

"Then I'll say goodbye. And leave you to your packing."

Twelve

Max locked himself into his suite for the next two days. He spoke to no one, saw no one. He didn't allow housekeeping in and instructed room service to leave his meals outside the door.

And like a caged beast, he prowled the empty suite night and day. He couldn't sleep. Every time he closed his eyes, he saw Janine's face. Heard her voice. She was haunting him and he was suffering for it.

"Damned woman."

He stalked across the living area and cursed silently because Janine's shoes weren't there for him to trip on. He hated going into the master bath because her creams and lotions and hair things weren't scattered across the red granite surface. He hated taking a shower because her bottles of shampoo and conditioner weren't crowded alongside his own. He hated going to bed because her scent still clung to her pillow and the wide mattress felt too damned empty to give him any peace.

He kept the stereo on, trying to shatter the quiet that felt as though it were choking him. He missed the sound of her voice, the peal of her laughter.

Damn it all to bloody hell, he missed *her*.

And that made him furious.

"Ridiculous," he muttered. "She lied to me. Claimed a pregnancy only to try to manipulate a different sort of marriage than the one she'd already turned down." It made no sense. None at all. Why would she do it? Why would she claim to be pregnant? What was the point? Where was the win?

Bugger it. Even when she wasn't around, Janine was making him insane. "Enough. I'm not a man to be led around by a woman. I got along fine without her before, I will again."

He stalked across the room to the French doors leading to the terrace, flung them open, stepped outside and took a deep breath of the brisk ocean air. But it didn't help. Nothing seemed to help. He curled his fingers over the rail, stared down at the pool below and in his mind's eye, saw Janine stretched out on one of the chaises.

The ghost of the woman was everywhere in this place. Grumbling, he went back inside. Back to the quiet, where only the soft sounds of light jazz played through the stillness. He hated being here and hated the thought of leaving, as well. For the first time in his life, Max felt unsettled and didn't care for it.

But holing up in this plush cave was not the answer and he knew it.

"Time to go home," he said, more to break up that annoying silence than for any other reason. "That's what's needed here. Home. Work. Soon enough, I'll forget all about her."

Nodding, he marched off to the bathroom, reached in and turned the shower knob. As steam filled the room, he turned, glanced into the quickly fogging mirror and saw the face of a man who looked haggard. This was what he'd come to? He stepped in closer to the counter, kicked the small trash can and cursed when it toppled over, spilling its contents across the tile floor.

"Bloody perfect," he muttered, bending down to clean up the mess.

On one knee, he paused and stared at the white plastic stick that had fallen facedown from the trash. Pregnancy test. Everything in him went still and cold. He shouldn't even look, he told himself. There was no need. He knew she wasn't pregnant. Knew it was all a ploy.

And yet...

He reached for it, saw the plus sign and felt his world shift.

"She *is* pregnant." Max stood up slowly, staring down at the stick that had changed everything for him. She was carrying his child and he'd sent her away because he hadn't trusted her.

Behind him, the shower roared and steam billowed out into the room. He looked into the nearly completely fogged mirror and saw only a ghostly reflection of himself. Appropriate, he thought, because without Janine there, he was bound to admit that he felt only partially alive.

The pregnancy notwithstanding, it was *she* whose absence tore at him. She who lived in his mind, his thoughts. She who Max had treated so badly she'd run from him.

And the question facing him now was what was he to do about it?

Was he going to go back to England, let Janine and their child slip away from him? Or would he risk everything and take a chance on finding something worth having?

Max reached out, swiped one hand across the fogged mirror and stared hard into his own eyes. There, he saw the answer he was looking for.

A week back from Fantasies and Janine was finding her feet again. She'd slipped into her life and let the familiar rhythm of it all soothe away the sharp edges of her memories.

Of course, Max still zipped through her thoughts at every unguarded moment. Which was both sad and infuriating. Her heart hurt, reminding her always of the emptiness that she'd be living with for the rest of her life. But beneath that soul-deep ache was the realization that because of the baby she carried, she'd always have a piece of Max with her. The best part of him. And eventually, she told herself, she'd get past the sting of his rejection. The fact that he hadn't believed her. Trusted her.

The fact that he hadn't wanted her love.

"Okay, Janine, enough thinking. Just focus on the job," she whispered, reaching for a fishbowl-shaped vase from the upper shelf in the design room of the flower shop. The plain concrete floor was strewn with discarded leaves and dead flower heads. Small puddles of water formed in the corners and the overhead skylight allowed sunlight to pour in.

Grabbing fistfuls of lavender sweet peas, pink tulips and soft white baby's breath, she set them aside, picked up the floral Styrofoam and soaked it thoroughly at the sink. Then she aligned it in the bottom of the vase and set to work. This arrangement was only the first of fifty that had to be prepared for an elegant wedding the following day. She had plenty to do to keep her busy, keep her mind off the fact that the man she had wanted to marry hadn't been interested.

Music played and she danced in place to the rock music pulsing through the sound system. Smiling, Janine focused only on color, design, the art of what she did. The sweet scent of fresh flowers filled the air and she found peace, as she could nowhere else.

While she worked, she heard the clang of the cowbell that hung over the front door of the shop and, only slightly irritated, she dried her hands on a shop towel and headed to the front of the store. She was the only one there at the moment, since the owner was out to lunch and their second designer wouldn't be in until later.

"Can I help—" She stopped speaking as she rounded the corner and found Max standing in the center of the small elegant shop.

He looked fabulous, of course. Black slacks, dark blue long-sleeved shirt and God, she'd forgotten just how dark his eyes were. Surrounded by flowering plants, hanging baskets and huge tubs of single flowers, Max stared at her as if seeing her for the first time.

And she was so tempted to cross the room, throw her arms around his neck and feel him hold her. But what would that solve, really? The issues that had splintered their faux relationship still existed. Nothing had changed.

But then, she wondered, why was he here?

"Janine—"

"Max, you shouldn't have come."

"No, you're wrong," he said and took a single step before stopping again when she backed up. "I should have come sooner. Better, I should never have let you leave Fantasies without me."

"But you did."

"Yes," he said, nodding, grim faced, his eyes unreadable, his features closed to her. "I did. And I'll spend the rest of my life trying to make it up to you for that piece of shortsightedness."

Janine's insides twisted and her heart ached. Just looking at him reminded her of everything she could never have. Having him here would only make it harder for her to forget him.

"Max, what're you doing here?"

"I'm an idiot."

She laughed shortly.

Max took a breath and decided he'd accept that short laugh of hers as a good omen. He needed to tell her everything he was thinking, feeling. He needed to take the biggest risk of his life and hope to hell he hadn't bollixed it all up by being an ass.

"I know that already, but thanks," she said drily.

"I thought you should know that now *I* know it as well."

"Thanks for the share, but I have to go back to work."

"No, don't." He walked to her quickly, sensing that she was going to turn her back on him before he'd had the chance to try to make this right. "Wait. Please. At least hear me out."

She looked down at the hand on her arm and didn't look away until he'd released her.

"Fine," she said then. "Talk."

He scraped one hand across his jaw, pulled in air like a drowning man and blurted, "I should have believed you. Should have known all along that you weren't the kind of woman I was used to dealing with."

"Yeah, but—"

"But I didn't want to trust my instincts where you were concerned. I thought my desire for you was clouding my thinking." She only stared at him and Max wondered how he'd ever thought to live without looking into her eyes. "I didn't want to risk believing in you. In *us*."

"Max," she said, and her voice was so low, he nearly missed it entirely. "It's too late. Don't you get it? We had our shot and we blew it." Shaking her head, she fought a sheen of tears with furious blinking and said, "It wasn't all your fault. I never should have taken you up on that bargain. Because I did, you figured I was no better than Lizzie."

"No. No, that wasn't it," he said and he risked putting hands on her again. Laying both hands on her shoulders, he felt the tension in her and cursed himself for ever having hurt her. "It wasn't about you, Janine. It was me. I was just the type of man you accused me of being. I never looked beyond my own safety zone. Never wanted to trust because that would mean I would have to risk myself again. Never wanted love because I didn't feel lovable. Stupid, really. And not much of an apology. But there it is."

"Max…"

"I would've been here sooner," he blurted, when he sensed that she was going to tell him to go away. "But first, I went home. To London. I bought a flower shop—it's quite near my company's downtown headquarters. Lovely place, really. You'd like it."

"Why would you buy a shop, Max?"

"For you." He lifted one hand to smooth his palm over her cheek, feel the line of her jaw, the slide of her skin beneath his again. God, how he'd missed her. "I bought the shop for you, Janine. I can't stay in California. My business is in Europe. But I can't do without you, either. I want you to come home with me, Janine. To England. I want you to marry me. I want you to love me. And blast it, I want to love you."

She swayed in his grasp. "Max..."

"Let me finish, get it all said, then you decide." He bent down, kissed her hard and quick, then looked directly into her eyes. "I'm not doing this because of the baby—"

Her gaze flickered.

"Yes," he said. "I believe you. I found the test strip."

"Oh."

"But a part of me believed you even before I found it," he said quickly, desperately. "The part of me that wanted to love you. The part of me that recognized you as the other part of myself from that very first night."

A solitary tear rolled down her cheek and he smoothed it away with the pad of his thumb. "Don't cry, Janine. I don't want to make you cry. Ever again. Just say you'll believe me. Say you'll let me be a part of your life. Be a part of our child's life. Say you still love me."

She took a great gulp of air and blew it out in a rush. "I do, Max. Of course I do, it's just—"

"No," he said it quickly and framed her face with his palms. "Don't qualify it. You showed me that love's a gift, Janine. One I was almost too stupid to appreciate. I'll never make that mistake again. I swear it to you."

She watched him and as the seconds ticked past, Max held his breath. At last, she smiled up at him and whispered in a tear-choked voice, "I do love you."

He grinned and felt better than he ever had in his life.

This was what he'd been missing. This was what he had so needed. Janine. She was all. She was everything.

"And I love you. Come home with me," he urged, pulling her into his arms. "Come to London. Marry me. Be with me. I promise you, with your help, I'll be the husband you deserve."

Janine looked up at him, felt the solid warmth of his arms around her and knew that the love she'd found at Fantasies had become real. It was everything she'd ever wanted. More than she'd ever dreamed of.

Wrapping her arms around his middle, Janine stared up into those fathomless dark eyes and went with her instincts. "Yes, Max. Yes, I'll marry you. I'll live in London. And I will love you for the rest of my life."

"Thank God," he said with a smile. Lowering his head to hers, he claimed a kiss to seal their new bargain. Their Till Death Do Us Part bargain.

The bargain that had been born in Fantasies.

* * * * *

Don't miss the final
REASONS FOR REVENGE
in CAPTURED BY THE BILLIONAIRE,
available October 2007
from Silhouette Desire.

Silhouette Desire

There was only one man for the job—
an impossible-to-resist maverick
she knew she didn't dare fall for.

MAVERICK
(#1827)

BY *NEW YORK TIMES* BESTSELLING AUTHOR
JOAN HOHL

"Will You Do It for One Million Dollars?"

Any other time, Tanner Wolfe would have balked at being
hired by a woman. Yet Brianna Stewart was desperate to
engage the infamous bounty hunter. The price was just
high enough to gain Tanner's interest...Brianna's beauty
definitely strong enough to keep it. But he wasn't about
to allow her to tag along on his mission. He worked
alone. Always had. Always would. However, he'd never
confronted a more determined client than Brianna. She
wasn't taking no for an answer—not about anything.

Perhaps a million-dollar bounty was not the only thing
this maverick was about to gain....

Look for MAVERICK

Available October 2007 wherever you buy books.

Ria Sterling has the gift—or is it a curse?—
of seeing a person's future in his or her
photograph. Unfortunately, when detective
Carrick Jones brings her a missing person's
case, she glimpses his partner's ID—and
sees imminent murder. And when her vision
comes true, Ria becomes the prime suspect.
Carrick isn't convinced this beautiful woman
committed the crime...but does he believe
she has the special powers to solve it?

Look for

Seeing Is Believing

by

Kate Austin

Available October
wherever you buy books.

HARLEQUIN®
NeXt™

www.TheNextNovel.com

HN88144

ATHENA FORCE

Heart-pounding romance and thrilling adventure.

A deadly masquerade

As an undercover asset for the FBI, mafia princess
Sasha Bracciali can deceive and improvise at a
moment's notice. But when she's cut off from
everything she knows, including her FBI-agent
lover, Sasha realizes her deceptions have masked
a painful truth: she doesn't know whom to trust.
If she doesn't figure it out quickly, her most
ambitious charade will also be her last.

Look for

CHARADE
by *Kate Donovan*

*Available in October
wherever you buy books.*

nocturne™

Look for
NIGHT MISCHIEF
by
NINA BRUHNS

Lady Dawn Maybank's worst nightmare
is realized when she accidentally conjures
a demon of vengeance, Galen McManus. What
she doesn't realize is that Galen plans to teach
her a lesson in love—one she'll never forget....

DARK
ENCHANTMENTS

▲

Available October wherever you buy books.

*Don't miss the last installment of Dark Enchantments,
SAVING DESTINY by Pat White, available November.*

HARLEQUIN®

Mediterranean NIGHTS™

Sail aboard the luxurious Alexandra's Dream and experience glamour, romance, mystery and revenge!

Coming in October 2007...

AN AFFAIR TO REMEMBER

by
Karen Kendall

When Captain Nikolas Pappas first fell in love with Helena Stamos, he was a penniless deckhand and she was the daughter of a shipping magnate. But he's never forgiven himself for the way he left her—and fifteen years later, he's determined to win her back.

Though the attraction is still there, Helena is hesitant to get involved. Nick left her once...what's to stop him from doing it again?

COMING NEXT MONTH

SDCNM0907